THE TROUBLE WITH BERNIE

Sharon Bushell

Sharon Bushell

For Julynn with best wishes!

Dream it. Do it.

SHARON BUSHELL

THE TROUBLE WITH BERNIE

ILLUSTRATED BY KATIE MILLER

Road Tunes Media
Homer, Alaska
2004

ROAD TUNES MEDIA
Homer, Alaska 99603
http://www.berniejones.com

Cover Design by Road Tunes Media
Cover Art Work by Katie Miller and W.B. Hughes
Manufactured in the United States of America
Worzalla - Stevens Point, Wisconsin

October 2004 First Edition

10 9 8 7 6 5 4 3 2 1

Library of Congress Cataloging-in-Publication Data
Bushell, Sharon The Trouble With Bernie
Summary: Bernie finds himself involved in many humorous and learning adventures in the 1950s.
1. Children's stories. (1. Friends- Fiction. 2. Pets-Fiction 3. 1950s - Fiction.
4. Humor - Fiction)
I. Title. p. 160 33 b/w drawings. Illustrated by Miller, Katie

ISBN 0-9721725-2-1
LCCN: 2004097474

http://www.berniejones.com

For Sam and Libby,
the Alex and Bernie
of my heart ...

Contents

The Initiation

A long time ago, in the 1950s, there lived a ten-year-old boy named Bernie Jones. He was a chubby, cheerful boy with unruly hair and a great big smile. He lived in a small town, in a big house, with his mom and dad, and his nine-year-old sister, Charmaine.

In a lot of ways, Bernie was lucky. He had a pretty good bike, a new pogo stick, and his best friend, Alex, lived next door. But the unlucky thing about Bernie was ... no matter where he went, no matter what he did, he always got into trouble.

Partially that is because Bernie loved insects. He kept worms in his shirt pocket and potato bugs in the cuffs of his pants. When he found a particularly beautiful bug, he would - without thinking - bring it into the house, to show his mother, even though he knew she disapproved of bugs.

He was so proud of them, one time he brought his entire collection of beetles to school, for show and tell. But somehow they all escaped, into every corner of the classroom, which caused the girls to scream and the boys to roar with laughter. Miss Jamison, dear, sweet Miss Jamison, for whom Bernie would gladly walk barefoot on red hot coals, was so flustered, she sent him to the principal's office-where he got into another big bunch of trouble.

Even more than he loved worms and bugs, Bernie loved snakes. And in this, again, he was lucky because right across the street from his house was a field with a lot of tall grass, and in the grass lived more garter snakes than any boy could ever hope to catch. On many spring and summer days, Bernie and Alex would go on snake safari. Over the years they had caught hundreds - maybe thousands - of the wriggling, writhing reptiles.

But no matter how many they caught, the boys always took the time to hold each snake up close, to admire its sleek, slim smoothness. Some snakes they recognized from previous catchings. To some they even gave names. Each one they returned to the tall grass, grateful to have held it, happy to let it slither away.

One time, early in the morning, Bernie made the mistake of bringing a really remarkable red racer home to show his sister, Charmaine. But she panicked and screamed so loud, she woke up the entire house and, once again, through no fault of his own, Bernie ended up in trouble.

The neighborhood in which Bernie and Alex lived was a

good one, not just because it had a whole lot of snakes; it also had a whole lot of kids, boys in particular. Most of them were twelve, thirteen or fourteen years old, and they always had a club that Bernie and Alex - because they were only ten years old - were not allowed to join. The club had disbanded and rebanded many times over the years and they always chose exotic sounding names. The Cobras. The Scorpions. The Amazing Men From Mars. Right now the name of their club was the Blazing Bandits, and more than anything in the world, Bernie and Alex longed to be Blazing Bandits.

No matter what the big boys called themselves, Clark Olsen was always the president of the club, and Brian Shaunessey was always number two in command. Both of them were fourteen years old, athletic, cool and confident. The twelve-year-old Patterson twins, Richard and Robert, and thirteen-year-old Larry Rustalio made up the rest of the gang. Over the years they had worked out an elaborate system of handshakes and signals. They took great pleasure in dropping just enough hints about their club that Bernie and Alex always wanted to join.

Cleverly, the big boys would let the word leak out about where they were holding their next secret meeting. Then, when the younger boys came sniffing around, they would bombard them with rotten apples, or giant pine cones, or squirt them with garden hoses.

In spite of the punishment they took and the fools they made of themselves, it was still the fondest desire of both Bernie and Alex, to be invited to join the Blazing Bandits. Little did they know that very soon their wish was going to come true.

When Clark Olsen found out that Alex Appleby's parents were buying the old Lincoln Theater, an idea ignited in Clark's teenage brain, like fireworks on the Fourth of July. In full panoramic color, he imagined Mr. Appleby giving his son enough free movie passes that Alex would then pass them along to other kids. Kids he wanted to get in good with. Clark imagined free popcorn being passed to him over the counter. Maybe he could even get a part-time job. If Alex felt indebted to him, maybe Mr. Appleby would hire Clark to be an usher at the theater. That would really dazzle the many girls on whom he had a crush.

To get the ball rolling, Clark called an emergency meeting of the Blazing Bandits. After school they met in the old abandoned shack in the neighborhood apple orchard. When all the members of the club arrived, Clark banged his gavel against the clubhouse wall and spoke in an authoritative tone. "Knock it off, you birdbrains! Let's get right to the point. I've been thinking ... it's about time we brought a new guy into our club. I nominate Alex Appleby."

The other four boys exchanged looks of shock and surprise, for this truly was an outrageous suggestion. One of the best parts of being a Blazing Bandit, or a Scorpion, or an Amazing Man from Mars, was keeping other kids out of the club.

The truth - and they didn't want anyone else to know this - was that they didn't really do all that much at their meetings, except read comics and argue a lot. Plus, if they let Alex Appleby in their club, they would also have to allow Bernie Jones in too, because Alex never did anything without Bernie. So there'd be not one but two ten-year-olds in their midst. There'd be nobody in the neighborhood to exclude.

Clark Olson wasn't worried. Now that he knew Alex Appleby's potential value as a Blazing Bandit, he wasn't about to let any of these bozos ruin his plan. He whacked the gavel against the flimsy plywood wall of the clubhouse, then paused a moment to make his voice come out calm and cool. "For as long as we've had a club, Bernie and Alex have wanted to join it. I say it's time we gave them a chance. I move that we let them join."

Brian Shaunessey jumped to his feet. "No way! Not a chance! Think about it ... they're practically babies! We can't associate with ten-year-olds!"

"Yeah, that's right," echoed the Patterson twins, who were at that moment racing midget cars on their knees, making motor noises out the sides of their mouths.

Larry Rustalio was rifling through the brown paper bag which held his leftovers from lunch. At that moment his mouth was stuffed with a big hunk of chocolate-covered cherry cake, so all he could do was nod his head in agreement with the twins.

"Listen you guys!" said Clark. "I'm the president of this club. I've always been the president of this club, and I'm telling you, this is a good opportunity."

He opened his mouth to say more, but at that moment Brian Shaunessey and the Patterson twins spontaneously jumped onto Larry Rustalio, and tried to wrestle the remains of the cherry cake out of his hands and into their mouths. Their club meetings often fell into chaos such as this.

"Order! I call for order!" Clark insisted, beating his gavel on the wall, on the floor, on the palm of his hand. When order was not restored, he frowned and beat the gavel harder. Then to demonstrate his authority, he stood straight up, forgetting that the clubhouse was less than five feet tall.

For Clark to bang his head was a personal victory for the other four boys. They hooted and howled with laughter. They pointed their fingers and rolled around on the floor, hands over their stomachs, laughing hysterically, which really made Clark mad. He could already feel the goose egg rising on the top of his head. Blinking back tears of shame and pain, he said, "You guys make me sick. Just look at you, rolling around on the floor, cackling like a bunch of hens. I'm trying to take care of some serious business here, and all you can do is fool around."

That prompted a whole new round of laughter from the four boys. Clark was not amused. "We might as well bring in a couple of ten-year-olds. They can prob'ly come up with better ideas than you guys can anyway, and obviously they've got you hands down when it comes to maturity."

The boys' laughter ended. "Are you calling us immature?" asked Robert Patterson.

"No," said Clark. "I'm saying ... you're a clown! And your brother is a clown. In fact, you're all a bunch of clowns!" He squeezed his face up into the tightest of frowns, folded his arms across his chest and glared at the other boys. Clark often had to assert himself in this fashion. He didn't really mind, though. He was practicing for the Marine Corps. He hoped to one day become a drill sergeant like his Uncle Joe.

Half an hour and seven votes later it was unanimous: Alex and Bernie were invited to join the big boys club. To insure this result, Clark had, one at a time, taken each boy behind the clubhouse and promised him a free movie pass in exchange for his vote. None of the boys had thought to question him, and Clark did not say where he was going to get the movie passes.

Later that night Larry Rustalio leaked the news to Bernie while they were playing tetherball in the Rustalio's yard. Bernie's jaw dropped and his mouth hung wide open. Just to be included in a game of tetherball with one of the big boys was enough, but to be invited into the Blazing Bandits ... for a full five seconds Bernie was speechless. Then he managed to say, "You're kidding! I don't believe it! This is too good to be true!" He felt weightless, as though his body had taken flight.

Thanks to his mother's spectacular lunches and after school snacks, Larry Rustalio was twice the size of most boys. He frowned and gave the ball a mighty whack, spinning it around and around and around the pole. "Yeah, well don't get your hopes up," he told Bernie. "First you have to pass the initiation. And let me tell you ... it isn't gonna be easy."

Larry's words were meant to strike terror in Bernie's heart, but Bernie was way beyond that. All he could think of was that his dream was coming true. He let the tether ball wrap itself around the pole and took off running as fast as he could to Alex's house.

Alex, like Bernie, was speechless at first, but not because he was happy. He scrunched up the entire left side of his face to get his eyeglasses to slide back into place. Alex had concerns. He had questions. "What about the initiation?" he asked. "You know how mean those guys can be. What if they make us walk the Patterson's picket fence blindfolded? What if they dress us up like girls and make us go to the Five and Dime?"

Over the years many legends had sprung up about the initiation rites of the big boys clubs. Supposedly one time a kid was forced on a midnight march, to swim naked in the freezing water of Peabody Creek. Rumor had it, another kid had to spend a night all alone in the cemetery near a freshly dug grave.

The big boys were hard to pin down about the specifics of

these events. When asked to name the names of these unsuccessful initiates, they grew silent and serious, and kept to the Blazing Bandit pledge of secrecy.

“I don’t know, Bern,” Alex said, “it seems to me like ... something’s fishy about this deal.” Ever the optimist, Bernie’s response was, “Don’t worry, Alex. Everything’s gonna be just fine.”

✻✻✻✻✻✻✻✻✻✻✻

The following Saturday dawned bright and beautiful. Bernie awoke with a smile on his face. It was a perfect day to be initiated into the Blazing Bandits. From now on he and Alex would be included whenever the big boys went hiking or camping, or swimming at the public pool. They’d be in on all the basketball games and baseball games, and they’d finally get to learn the secret handshakes and passwords - all the really cool stuff.

But Alex was not so sure. He looked perfectly all right when Bernie showed up at his door that morning, but what he said was, “I’ve kinda got a stomach ache, Bern. Do you think maybe the guys’ll let us wait ‘til next week?”

“Nnnn, I doubt it,” Bernie answered. “Something tells me this is a once in a lifetime opportunity. If we blow it, they’ll probably never let us join.”

Alex frowned and nodded in agreement. He knew what Bernie said was true. His dad had just spent a whole month convincing his mother that they should buy the old Lincoln

Theater. Alex had heard plenty of talk about once in a lifetime opportunities.

And so it was that Bernie, light of heart and high of hope, and Alex, full of doubt and dread, headed out the door toward their rendezvous. The big boys had told them to arrive at the far corner of the apple orchard at high noon and not to tell any of the other kids ... or else.

All the other boys were already there. The Patterson twins were rolling around on the ground, trying to stuff squished and rotting apples down each other's shirts. Larry Rustalio was eating an enormous three-layer sandwich and staring off into space. Clark Olsen and Brian Shaunessey were deep in conversation, their backs turned to the other boys. At their feet was something that Bernie and Alex could not quite see.

"Well, well, well," said Clark, when he turned and spotted the two younger boys. "There they are, the newest members of our club. That is, if they're in the mood for eating ... mayonnaise!" He stepped aside and there at his feet were two giant jars.

The Patterson twins stopped their scuffling around and

Larry swallowed his last bite of sandwich. This was an unexpected treat. Clark had been promising for years, that someday he would force someone to eat a whole jar of mayonnaise. Now, in addition to a free movie pass, they would finally get to see this much-awaited spectacle. They shoved each other aside to get a better look.

Clark was pleased to have the undivided attention of all the boys. Even though he appeared calm, cool and collected, he had passed a restless night and had come to the conclusion that maybe this wasn't such a great idea after all. What if there were no free movie passes? What if these two new guys brought scorn or ridicule to the club? Clark had stared at the luminous dial of his alarm clock as the minutes ticked into hours. By morning he had come up with a solution. If Bernie and Alex disappointed him in any way, he would simply expel them. Throw them out of the club. Tell them it had all been a joke. So, really, there was no way he could lose.

"As I was saying, all you guys have to do is each eat a jar of this wonderful, delicious mayonnaise and you'll become the newest members of the Blazing Bandits."

Bernie could not believe his luck. He loved mayonnaise! It was one of his favorite things. But it was bad luck for Alex, who had a delicate stomach and, whenever possible, avoided such things. He liked his sandwiches plain: cheese and baloney, with nothing added, or good old peanut butter and jam.

"Here ya go, boys." Clark handed Bernie and Alex each

a jar and a spoon. He had not revealed his true motive for wanting Bernie and Alex in the club. Word had not yet gotten out that the Applebys were buying the theater. Clark's mother, a real estate agent, was among the first to know.

"All right, you two," he said, "you have to finish off the whole jar. No stopping. On your mark, get set, GO!"

This was not Bernie's favorite brand of mayonnaise, but he didn't really mind. Tablespoon after tablespoon, he happily gobbled down the gooey white stuff. The initiation was a lot easier than he figured it would be. In his mind he saw himself hitting a fly ball clear out of the neighborhood field, way beyond the reach of any of the big boys. He imagined lazy afternoons at the swimming pool, impressing all the teenagers with how well he could dog paddle.

Alex's thoughts were not nearly so lofty. He visualized how much his stomach would have to expand in order to accommodate an entire jar of mayonnaise. He was a lot smaller than Bernie; his insides couldn't hold as much. He scooped out the tiniest of bites and forced it into his mouth. According to what Clark had said, as long as he didn't stop, he wasn't breaking the rules.

Alex stole a glance at Bernie, who was halfway done with his jar and showed no sign of slowing down. Bernie had many outstanding qualities. He was loyal. He was trustworthy. He loved bugs and worms and snakes. But the way he tackled that jar of mayonnaise, without struggle or complaint, made Alex admire him more than ever.

Bernie was in heaven. This initiation was a cinch! Soon all the secrets of the Blazing Bandits would be revealed to him: the special handshakes, the coded messages, every sacred thing. In his heart he vowed that whatever was involved with being a member of the club, he would keep the secrets well. He would show these guys that a ten-year-old was worthy after all.

Bernie was almost done with his jar but Alex still had a long way to go when he started feeling woozy. *Uh oh*, he thought, *this is serious. This is bad. This is really really bad.* With every tiny spoonful he forced into his mouth, Alex thought the word *mayonnaise* until it lost all meaning, lost every bit of sense. He tried to think of how to spell it, M A Y O ... what was next? He was a championship speller; he could outspell any of the big boys. But right now the word was so distasteful, so repulsive, all it meant was goo, slime ... sick.

The taste in his mouth went from bad to worse. As Bernie was spooning out the last of his jar, Alex was running for the bushes. The mayonnaise was coming back up, and along with it, his longtime dream of becoming a Blazing Bandit.

The big boys thought this was funny as could be; they all stood around howling with laughter. The Patterson twins, who were easily amused, were once again rolling around on the ground, holding their sides, laughing 'til tears streamed down their faces. Brian and Clark were also delighted; anything for a laugh, as long as it was at someone else's expense.

Only one boy offered to help Alex: Bernie, of course. He patted Alex's shoulder and said, "It'll be all right. It's okay. I just wish there was something I could do to help."

Then came the voice of Clark Olsen, shouting above the laughter. "There *is* something you can do, Bernie. You can eat the rest of his mayonnaise."

Just hearing the word was enough for Alex. He had to duck down behind the bushes and get sick again. There was more laughter and shouting, then Bernie was dipping his spoon into the second jar.

Time seemed to slow down. The boys' voices got softer and softer until they almost seemed to fade away. Bernie felt all floaty and strange. He knew for sure that he did not want to

eat another jar of mayonnaise. But he knew something else for sure too, something about himself. He had seen it in the eyes of his best friend when he patted him on the shoulder. He didn't know what it was, but it was something real, something powerful. And right now, if he had to, Bernie Jones would eat a dozen quarts of mayonnaise; he would eat all the mayonnaise in the world. He and Alex would become Blazing Bandits ... nothing could stop them now.

All the big boys were thoroughly dazzled by Bernie's accomplishment. They hadn't believed it was possible, that anyone could pass the mayonnaise test. Now they had a guy in their club who could eat two whole quarts. That might come in handy in the future, for pie-eating contests and dares from kids in other clubs.

"I've never seen anything like this before," said Brian Shaunessey. "We should've let him in the club a whole lot sooner."

"Yeah," said Clark Olsen. "Just look at him go."

As Bernie scooped out the last spoonful, a cheer went up from the crowd. Then all the boys rushed over to him, to congratulate him and shake his hand. Larry Rustalio even asked him for his autograph.

But Bernie did not let the attention go to his head. He made sure that Alex was okay, then both of them were ushered into the clubhouse, and the future they had dreamed of for so long began. The secret handshakes were demonstrated. The passwords and coded messages were explained. Plans were made for a hike next Saturday down to the depths of Peabody Gulch. Then the meeting broke up and all the kids hurried home for lunch.

Bernie Jones wasn't in the mood to eat, though. He wouldn't be for the whole rest of the day. Instead he walked Alex home, then he climbed to the top of the big apple tree in his backyard. There he looked out over the town and enjoyed the glow of his accomplishment. Not only had he become a Blazing Bandit; half a day had passed already and he hadn't even gotten into any trouble. And though his stomach *did* feel kind of gurgly, Bernie figured that, whatever else happened to him the whole rest of his life, he would never ever feel this good again.

The Beehive

Bernie sat on his front steps, staring out at the sky, trying to think up a really good idea. Tomorrow was his turn for show and tell, and he wanted to do something really spectacular. Something no one would ever forget. He thought about how, for her show and tell, MaryAnn Hastings had brought in her dog, Sweetie Pie, a big white poodle. Sweetie Pie had barked on command, sat, jumped, twirled around in a circle, and then walked on her hind legs the whole length of the classroom. MaryAnn bragged that Sweetie Pie was a pure bred, which made her better and smarter than other dogs. Bernie had once brought his own dog, Weezer, to school for show and tell, but the experience had been far from successful. It was, in fact, painful to remember.

Way, way high up in the sky, a jet was flying by. Bernie leaned his head back and followed the white trail it left behind, and that is when he saw it: a beehive, a small, tidy,

beehive, just about the size of a canteloupe and pretty much hidden under the eaves of the porch.

A beehive! That would be the perfect thing to bring to school. He sat there for a long time, staring up at it, waiting to see if any bees came out. He told himself that if any had, he wouldn't dare touch it, much less bring it to show and tell. But fortunately, after carefully observing it for a full ten minutes, Bernie didn't see a single bee. Oh boy! This was perfect! No one had ever brought a beehive to school before.

He went to the garage, got a ladder, climbed up to the top of the porch, and carefully removed the hive from where it hung. He held it in his hands, put his eyeball up to the hole, and peered inside. Nope, no activity. It was definitely an abandoned nest.

So, it was all settled. Tomorrow he would bring it to school, and his show and tell would be a huge success. He took the hive, along with the ladder, and left it in the garage where he would retrieve it tomorrow on his way to school.

That night, as he was drifting off to sleep, Bernie pictured himself showing the hive off to his fourth grade class. He had taken the time to study the encyclopedia, to read all about bees. He could now answer any questions the kids might ask. Miss Jamison, who loved all things from nature

- except for snakes and spiders - would be proud that Bernie had brought in something so interesting, and that he was so well prepared.

But his plan to dazzle Miss Jamison was foiled, because when Bernie walked into his classroom the next morning, Miss Jamison was not there. She was home sick, and the substitute teacher was - oh no! - the one and only Mrs. Broadbottom. Bernie felt a stab, not only of disappointment, but of dread. He didn't know why, but every time he was around Mrs. Broadbottom, he always seemed to have bad luck.

He placed the hive, which was in a brown paper bag, on one of the classroom shelves, then crossed his fingers and hoped for the best. Right away he felt better. Plus, he was wearing his lucky shirt, so he was pretty sure that things couldn't go too wrong.

"Good morning, class!" boomed Mrs. Broadbottom, as she took her place at the blackboard. She had a kind of half-smile, half-snarl on her face. "I would like you all to take out pencil and paper. Write your name clearly at the top of the page. We're going to have a spelling test." She folded her hands ever so gracefully at her waist and allowed a peaceful look to transform her face.

Geraldine McCutchin raised her hand and in a tiny voice said, "But Miss Jamison always gives us our spelling tests on Friday."

"Perhaps you hadn't noticed," said Mrs. Broadbottom, "but

I am not Miss Jamison. Also, you've had all these words before, so I'm sure you know them perfectly and won't have any trouble spelling them correctly." All the kids reached for pencil and paper.

"Ready? First word: trouble. As in, 'I do not want to annoy the teacher and get myself into trouble.'"

Pencil scratchings could be heard throughout the classroom.

"Second word: punished. If I get into trouble, I expect to be punished.

"Third word: apologize. A good child is quick to apologize."

The spelling lesson went on and on. As Mrs. Broadbottom walked around the classroom, she tapped a ruler into the palm of her hand and sometimes sliced it in the air in front of herself, like a sword, as though at any second she might lash out and strike the nearest child. Mrs. Broadbottom prided herself on her ability to handle a classroom. She had been a substitute teacher for a long time, and she knew how to inspire terror in children of all ages. She considered it a compliment, that all the kids cringed whenever she was near.

When the test was over and all the papers had been passed to the front, Mrs. Broadbottom announced, "Today, for show and tell, we have (she glanced at the note on her desk) Janeen Welshmeier and Bernie Jones. Janeen, would you like to go first?"

Janeen Welshmeier reached underneath her seat for a rectangular object, which she tried to conceal as she walked to the front of the room. It was a license plate. She smiled nervously and held it up for everyone to see. "This was made by my Uncle Roscoe. He lives in the state penitentiary. Whenever we go to Fairfield, we always visit him there."

Mrs. Broadbottom pulled a hankie from the front of her dress and swiped at her nose, something she always did when she felt uncomfortable.

"You've probably seen the prison," Janeen added. "It sits way up on a hill, when you first drive into the city. It looks like a great big house ... except it has barbed wire all around it."

Right away there was a hand waving from the back row. It was Chuckie Wadsworth. "What'd your uncle do?"

"He's a counterfeiter," said Janeen. "He used to be a burglar, but then a friend of his gave him a printing press. They set it up in his basement and started making hundred dollar bills. They got real rich."

"Wow," said Chuckie.

"Now he just makes license plates all day," said Janeen. "But when he gets out of prison, he's going to go to law school."

"Your uncle's a jailbird!" shouted one of the kids.

"He is not!" said Janeen. "And even if he is ... so what? My mom says that sometimes even nice people have to go to jail." She scrunched her nose up, snorted at the source of the unkind remark, and stomped back to her desk, her head held high. Several of the students wanted to see the license plate close up. All this made Mrs. Broadbottom extremely nervous.

She drew in a deep breath and said, "Well, that's all very nice. Thank you, Janeen. Now I think we should get on to our next student. I believe that would be (she checked the note on her desk again) Bernie Jones."

While Janeen was returning to her desk, Bernie dashed to the back of the room, grabbed the brown paper bag and walked to the front of the class.

"Today I have something very special to share with you," he said. "I found it under the roof of our porch." He withdrew the beehive and proudly held it up for the class to admire. "It's really cool, huh?"

The instant Mrs. Broadbottom saw what it was, she got a puckered up look on her face, sort of like a prune. "Merciful heavens!" she said, and began fanning herself with her hankie.

"Don't worry," said Bernie, who could tell she was kind of concerned. "There aren't any bees in it. I checked."

Nevertheless, Mrs. Broadbottom fanned herself vigorously and tucked a strand of silver hair back into place. Lately she had been experimenting with different hairdos and today she was wearing a large bun on the top of her head, not unlike the beehive which Bernie held in his hands.

He walked up and down the aisles to show the hive up close to each kid and answer everyone's questions. "There are a whole lot of bees in the world," Bernie explained. "To be exact, there are ten thousand different species of bees."

"Wow!" Alex exclaimed. He had no idea Bernie had such a great show and tell. Yesterday he had been all worried about it, so worried that he had declined a grasshopper hunt in Snake City, but this was really good!

The showing of the beehive had everyone's attention, and Bernie had to remind several of the boys not to touch it. It was fragile! He continued his explanation. "But, even though there are thousands of species of bees, there are only two kinds: the social kind and the solitary kind. The bees that came from this hive were social bees, the kind that make honey. A whole bunch of 'em used to live in here."

Bernie went on to explain the intricacies of how honey is made and how beekeeping as a hobby had become very popular. Two of the girls told him they thought the hive was beautiful. MaryAnn Hastings, angry because Bernie's show and tell was better than hers, tried not to be interested in the beehive, but even she had to take a good look at it. You never got to see one up this close.

It was hard for Bernie to do so much talking with such a big smile on his face, for he could not conceal his joy. The show and tell was a huge success. Maybe, when he got to be an adult, he would take up the hobby of keeping bees. He would wear a net over his head and collect the honey from the hives. It would be really neat.

"Ah, that's not anything so great!" said Chuckie Wadsworth, when Bernie reached his desk in the back row. Chuckie had his arms folded across his chest, frowning, pretending he didn't care to view the beehive. "I could get one of those things any time I want!"

Bernie had approached Chuckie cautiously. He was a big guy, but he could move fast, and often did. And just like that - even though he had been told not to - Chuckie reached out to touch the hive, causing it to fall to the floor and crack in two.

Chuckie withdrew his hand in horror, for he had not meant to destroy the hive. He just wanted to touch it, just for a second.

Bernie, who was crushed, heart and soul, at this terrible turn of events, bent down to pick up the beehive. When he did, he saw something he didn't expect to see. Bees! Lots and lots of bees! Dozens! Maybe hundreds! They were crawling out of the hive and onto the floor, and in the next moment they all took to the air, flying around and around and around, buzzing to every corner of the room.

It was instant panic. Kids were screaming. Kids were shrieking. No one could stand still. They swatted at the bees and jumped on top of their desks, and ran to and fro, squealing. They'd all been trained what to do in case an atom bomb was dropped on their school, but when it came to a sudden invasion of bees, they were helpless.

Bernie wasn't screaming or running, he was just standing there, stunned beyond belief. How could this have happened? How could something go from being so good to so bad, so fast? And now what should he do?

If Miss Jamison had been there, she'd have gotten things under control, but Mrs. Broadbottom was too busy with her own problems to worry about those of her students. She was terrified of bees, and she too had climbed on top of her desk, for no good reason except that she had to do something. It turned out to be a big mistake though, because that made her, by far, the tallest of anyone in the room. Her gray hair, piled on top of her head and shaped very much like a hive, caught the attention of the buzzing bees. They were attracted too, by the sweet flowery scent of her Lily of the Valley cologne. One by one, they flew toward her head and landed on her hair and just stayed there.

It was the most remarkable sight that any of the kids had ever seen. They all stopped screaming and running and just stared in complete silence at Mrs. Broadbottom. She looked like she was wearing a black and yellow hat.

Despite her terrible fear, Bernice Broadbottom, who had once been a Girl Scout, knew a thing or two about bees. She became very, very still. She didn't move a muscle. She didn't even blink her eyes. She stared straight ahead and wished with all her might for lightning to strike the school, or any swift end to her misery.

Bernie knew he had to do something, and do it quick. He

walked to the front of the room, took hold of Mrs. Broadbottom's hand, helped her down from the desk, and lead her toward the door. All the other kids just stared in silence. Things like this didn't happen in real life - only on TV. Too panicked to resist, Mrs. Broadbottom let herself be guided by the boy she most wanted to strangle with her bare hands. One terrified step at a time, they made it to the door.

In hindsight, Bernie was never able to say exactly what it was he was thinking during the walk down the hall from the classroom to the exit. He was mostly just listening to the sound of Mrs. Broadbottom breathing and the soft, buzzing noise of the bees. So far not a single person had been stung, and even though Bernie knew he would soon be in trouble, he was thrilled to see so many bees up close. It was unfortunate, however, that they were on the teacher's head.

Their classroom was at the end of the hall, so they didn't have far to go. Bernie pushed the door open, and out they walked, into the sunshine of a warm spring day. As soon as they were outside, Mrs. Broadbottom started hopping up and down, waving her arms around and squealing all the squeals she had held back before. Her behavior was not consistent with her Girl Scout training, but she had been driven nearly mad by the sound and feel of bees all over her head and she could contain herself no longer.

The bees seemed to like it better outside, and a few of them started to fly away. There were a lot of them that remained though, so Bernie, seeing that there was a long stick, right there, laying on the ground, bent down, picked it up and started poking it at Mrs. Broadbottom's hair, to get the rest of the bees to leave. Whatever she had done to get her hair all knotted up like that, she had done a pretty good job, because Bernie had to poke and poke and poke before her hairdo finally collapsed and the rest of the bees flew away. By then, all the kids were outside, crowded around. They didn't want to miss this, which was by far the most spectacular event of their young lives.

Mrs. Broadbottom, as well as being terrified and enraged, had never been so humiliated in all her life. The children were laughing at her. Her hair was hanging in clumps. She turned to face Bernie with a murderous look in her eyes. She pointed to the ground next to her. "Come here," she demanded.

Bernie, who always obeyed his elders, knew it was time to run. He dashed through the circle of kids and ran for all he was worth. The catastrophe had just gotten ten times worse. Not only had he robbed all those bees of a home, now Mrs. Broadbottom would probably send him to the principal's office for the whole rest of his life.

"Come back here," she yelled. "You come back."

But Bernie did not come back. He ran to the far end of the playground, toward the shelter of the monkey bars.

Mrs. Broadbottom, who was an extra-large sort of person, picked up the stick Bernie had been using and took off after him like a streak of lightning. She ran like a wild animal. She ran faster than she had in decades.

Around and around the monkey bars she chased Bernie. Once, twice, she almost caught up with him. She had her stick held high, ready to give him a good whack with it. As fast as she was though, he was faster, and he managed to stay just beyond her reach.

Finally she got so tired, she came to a halt. Panting to catch her breath, preparing for one more try at him, Mrs. Broadbottom's eye caught the gleam of something shiny, something held by one of the students. It was Janeen Welshmeier, with the license plate still in her hand. That brought Mrs. Broadbottom's attention back to what really mattered.

What was it Janeen had said? That *sometimes even nice people have to go to jail?* Mrs. Broadbottom, too dizzy and exhausted to panic, merely wondered ... were there criminal penalties for trying to strike a student with a stick when the student so obviously deserved it? She imagined herself arguing in a court of law, that sometimes, under certain circumstances, a student truly deserved a good whacking. Then she thought about the Fairfield House of Corrections.

She had driven by it many times and she was quite certain that she did not want to live there.

Mrs. Broadbottom dropped the stick. She brushed her hair away from her eyes, adjusted the waistline of her dress, took a deep breath, and managed to say in a calm and almost cheerful voice, "Well, I guess that's enough excitement for one day. Let's all go back to class now, shall we?"

The kids were totally shocked. She sounded just like a regular teacher. They trailed along behind her as she headed back toward the school. Bernie, because he couldn't figure out what else to do, took his place at the end of the line. But he kept his distance, and watched Mrs. Broadbottom's every move, in case she went berserk again.

Mrs. Broadbottom spent the rest of the day staring out the window, fanning herself with her hankie and frowning. Now that things were under control, she felt no reason to demonstrate false cheer. She kept the class in at lunchtime and would not allow them to go outside at afternoon recess either. To keep them busy, *to take their minds off things*, she assigned them three chapters of geography and two extra math lessons. Bernie knew it was his fault they had so much work to do and that they didn't get any recess. He figured his show and tell had been a complete and utter flop. He did his lessons with his head resting on his arm, pushing his pencil in misery.

When the school day ended, he did his best to blend in with all the other kids as they hurried toward the door. He almost made it too, but then Mrs. Broadbottom was in his path, her eyes all squinted up and her hands on her hips. In her left hand she held a ruler. Bernie stopped dead in his tracks. All the other kids scurried out the door. "Well Bernie, it's been quite a day, don't you agree?" she asked, with that snarling smile on her face.

He gulped and said, "Yes ma'am."

She tapped the ruler ever so gently into the palm of her hand, looking him dead in the eyes. "We aren't going to have any more little incidents like that, ever again, are we?"

"No ma'am."

"Good," she added. "Let's shake on it." She put her hand out. Bernie hesitated. If he offered her his hand, she might whack it. She might grab it and twist it behind his back and snap his arm in two. But what could he do? He cringed and closed his eyes and gave her his hand. She pumped it up and down.

"You know ... I wasn't really going to hit you with that stick," she said, chuckling merrily. "It was just a little joke, to amuse the other students."

Bernie's eyes popped wide open. He was certain she had meant to whack him. He was positive, in fact. He opened his mouth to say so, but what came out was, "I'll never bring any more beehives to school again, ever."

"Nnnnn good," she said, no longer chuckling. "See that you don't." Then she squeezed his hand extra tight.

"Uh, I gotta go," said Bernie, snatching back his hand and hurrying for the door.

Chuckie Wadsworth was waiting for him outside. "Hey Bern," he said, "sorry about the beehive. Where'd ya find it anyway? Think there's another one around somewhere? I've got a really good idea, but I've gotta find a beehive."

Bernie looked over Chuckie's shoulder and he could see, all up and down the street, kids were pointing at him, and smiling and waving. He was a hero. Even with all the extra work the class had to do, his show and tell had been a success.

"I couldn't believe it," said Chuckie, "her whole head was covered with bees! Think you could get the same thing to happen again? 'Cause my sister ... I'd love it if my sister had a whole swarm of bees on her head. That'd show her."

Bernie shook his head. "Sorry, Chuckie, but I don't think I'm gonna be looking for any more bees for a long time."

Alex showed up then, just in time to say, "Yeah, if I were you Bern, I'd stick to snakes." He crinkled up his nose to adjust his eyeglasses. "Snakes are a lot more predictable."

Bernie nodded in agreement, and then they were off, two boys into a spring afternoon. Maybe they would catch snakes. Maybe they would play with Lincoln Logs. Maybe they would just stare at the sky. But always, for the whole rest of their lives, even if they lived to be a hundred years old, they would remember this day and the substitute teacher and the beehive.

Saturday at the Movies

Bernie Jones stood at his bedroom mirror and admired his brown vest, which had the words "Appleby's Theater" stitched in tiny letters on the pocket. He had a job! True, it was only for a few hours one day a week, but, as Grandpa Jones had proudly said, "That's how a feller gets started."

Mr. Appleby had hired Alex and Bernie to work on weekends. During and after the matinee they walked around the theater with flashlights and picked up trash and made sure everything was running smoothly.

Bernie took one more glance at himself in the mirror, then ran down the stairs, hollered out *goodbye!* to whoever was in the house, put on his jacket and began the half-mile walk to the theater.

He walked down Park Street, whistling happily, then made

a left turn on First Street. He liked to use this route because it took him past the public swimming pool. That way all the kids could see that he was on his way to work.

****

Five minutes after Bernie turned onto First Street, Clark Olsen slammed the door of his house, jammed his hands deep into his pockets and tromped down Park Street toward town. He didn't have a destination, he was just walking. Aimlessly, miserably walking. If it wasn't for the fact that he was fourteen years old - practically grown up - he felt like he might even cry, he felt so bad.

Clark kicked at the rocks on the sidewalk as he walked. For a long time his life had been pretty simple: home, school, sports and hanging out with the other guys in the neighborhood. Now it was getting more and more complicated all the time. He had always been at the top of his class, the best at everything, and for that reason he expected that he always would be. Thank goodness, from the outside looking in, it still seemed that way. He was still the best looking boy in eighth grade, still a basketball champion, still the president of the Blazing Bandits. But that wasn't enough anymore. Now life could only be complete if he had all that and Lisa Wondermore too.

The thought of Lisa Wondermore made Clark's heart flutter, and also made him kick wildly at another rock in his path. Because even though he was handsome and smart and popular and athletic, he was and always would be a whole year younger than Lisa Wondermore. Nothing, not one thing in the whole wide world could ever be done about that. Clark stroked his hand through the Brylcreamy smoothness of his hair. When he grew up and left town, he might go on to become a famous movie star or even president of the United States, but no matter what, he would never ever be older than Lisa Wondermore.

Clark sent another rock flying. It was so unfair! It was like there was an unwritten rule that older girls weren't supposed to be interested in younger guys.

The Wondermores had just moved to town. They had, in fact, moved into the neighborhood, into the old McGuire house. Lisa had a twelve-year-old brother, Joey, who so far no one knew anything about.

Each time Clark passed their house, he scanned the walkway, the porch, the yard, his eyes hungry for the sight of beautiful Lisa Wondermore. He had had many crushes in his life, but none like the one he had on Lisa.

Though it pained Clark to think of her, he recalled the sweetness of her smile. Sometimes, between classes, her gaze would fall on him for just a moment, and she would smile. In those blissful seconds he would think, *yes, there is hope for me*. The feeling was intoxicating. He would get all floaty, which would cause him to indiscriminately be nice to everyone, even kids who had no status at all. But more often than not, Lisa would look to the left of him, or to the right, and then everything, everything, the whole rest of the day, would be ruined.

He knew he was in love, he had no doubt of that. His older cousin Jerome had once told him, "The way you can tell if you're in love is, it feels like somebody just punched you right in the stomach."

****

Clark came over the crest of First Street just in time to see the lineup of kids outside Appleby's Theater. Wait a second. There was Lisa ... standing next to Eugene McElravy! They were together. It couldn't be! She was going to the movies with Eugene McElravy! He was in eighth grade, younger by two months than Clark himself. He squinted for a closer look. Eugene was standing still as a statue and smiling at Lisa, probably saying something he thought was real funny, and she ... she was laughing at him.

This was too much! Clark burned with fury. He felt like kicking the biggest rock he could find or smacking the nearest telephone pole. All the while he was getting closer to them, closer. They had spotted him. They were waving. He couldn't even cross the street now. They would guess. They would know. His mind raced. The record shop. That's it, the record shop; it was just beyond the theater.

“Hi Clark!” Lisa smiled at him and gave a little wave. “Hey,” was all Eugene had to say.

“Oh, hi!” Clark said. “I’m ... uh ... I’m on my way to the ... record store.”

Then the moment was over, and Clark was further down the street, past the theater, past the record shop, head down, heart broken. He didn’t even realize he’d passed the record shop until he was three stores down. And then he had to, he just had to, turn around and look, and yes, they were watching him. They had seen the great Clark Olsen, perhaps for the first time ever, lose his cool.

Clark was so flustered, he could hardly think. He ducked into the next shop, a soda fountain. “May I help you?” asked the girl behind the counter. “Yeah ... mmm ... I’ll take a root beer.” He didn’t even like root beer.

A few minutes later he was back on the street. All the people waiting in line for the movies were slowly drifting into the theater. The street was no longer crowded. Lisa and Eugene had already gone inside. Clark’s gaze fell onto the solitary figure of Bernie Jones.

To see Bernie, so happy, skipping down the street, irritated Clark to no end. He took a slurp of his root beer, shook his head in disgust at Bernie’s happiness, then remembered ... Bernie Jones worked at the theater. Bernie Jones could find out what the deal was with Lisa and Eugene.

Clark started running and shouting. “Hey Bern! Hey wait! Wait for me!”

****

Bernie was just about ready to open the door to the theater when he heard a familiar voice. Proud to be acknowledged in public by a fellow Blazing Bandit, Bernie took his hand off the door and waited for Clark.

“Here, Bern,” said Clark. “I, uh, I ... bought you a root beer.”

“Oh, thanks,” said Bernie. “But I get all the soda pop I want on account of that I work here.”

Clark’s smile turned to a sneer. “Duh! I know where you work, Bernie. That’s why I’m here. I came to ask you a favor.”

“Sure, I’ll do you a favor,” said Bernie. “What’dya need?” Bernie had an amazing ability to talk and never once stop smiling.

“Well,” said Clark. “It’s like this. I happen to know that Lisa Wondermore is at the movies with Eugene McElravy. And what I want from you (he thumped Bernie on the chest with his index finger when he said the word ‘you’) is to watch and see what they do. Watch where they sit. Try to listen to what they talk about. You know. You know what I mean.”

“Sure,” said Bernie. “I understand. I’ll watch ‘em for you.”

152
THE
BLOB

“Good,” said Clark. “Because I’ll be waiting right here when you get off work. Right in this spot.” He pointed to the pavement beneath his feet. “And I want you to tell me everything.” Again he thumped Bernie on the chest with his finger. “I want to know every (thump) single (thump) thing (thump).”

Clark gazed long and menacingly into Bernie’s eyes, took a loud slurping sip from the root beer, then turned around and walked away. Bernie put his hand back on the theater door, opened it, and stepped inside.

****

Instantly he was absorbed into his other life, his professional life. He felt a stab of joy so profound it was all he could do to contain it: the smell of popcorn, the smell of hot dogs, the dark of the theater, the plush thickness of the stained carpet, the shouting of hundreds of kids. And he, he was not just another moviegoer, he was an employee! He got to pick up the trash. He got to run errands for the guy in the projection booth. The whole place, practically, was his.

Bernie walked over to the snack bar, greeted the high school girl named Wendy who worked there, took off his jacket and reached for the broom and dust pan. He was official now, officially at work, on the lookout for every speck of popcorn, every ticket stub, every empty box that littered the lobby. His happiness was complete.

But Bernie did not forget the favor Clark had asked of him. Every now and then he glanced up from his sweeping and tracked the movements of Eugene McElravy and Lisa Wondermore. For a long time they stood in line at the snack bar. Bernie carefully noted that they talked some, they laughed some, but mostly they did nothing at all. When they reached the front of the line, Bernie came back around the counter to see what candy and pop choices they would make, so he could report it to Clark later on. Lisa got Junior Mints and a small root beer. Eugene went for the Good and Plentys - a big box - and a jumbo 7 Up. Then the music from the newsreel started, and the two of them moved, along with the swarms of other kids, into the theater.

Bernie grabbed a flashlight and told Wendy he'd see her later. He had to go check out the theater to make sure everything was okay.

In the darkness that enveloped him, Bernie clicked on his flashlight. He kept it pointed at the floor, walked down the long aisle to the front row, all the way across, then back up the other side. From the mini-lights on each outside seat, Bernie could tell which group of kids was which, and who was who, and what was going on. He made several trips through and around, walking slowly, one eye on the newsreel, one eye on the kids, always on the lookout for a stray popcorn bag, an empty box, a squashed paper cup.

Eugene and Lisa, instead of sitting in front, where Bernie and his friends always sat, were in the very back row, kind of in the middle, not the easiest place for Bernie to watch them. Nevertheless, to the best of his ability, he did. They were not the least bit interesting. They talked. They laughed. They ate their candy and drank their pop. It was pretty boring stuff. Why did Clark even care what they did?

The newsreel ended and the previews began. Oh boy, here was a show Bernie couldn't wait to see, "The Blob." It was a big, quivering mass of something that looked like green Jello, only it ate people, just swallowed them right up, which made it get bigger and bigger.

As Bernie took a few more steps toward the rear of the theater, he quickly looked at Eugene and Lisa, not expecting to see anything. Instead he got the shock of his life.

They were holding hands! And then, as though they had planned it in advance, just to shock Bernie even more, Lisa Wondermore and Eugene McElravy turned to face each other, leaned in closer, and exchanged a kiss.

A kiss! Bernie's mouth dropped open, his feet stopped walking and he sucked in a whole chest full of air. Although he hadn't been instructed to, and even though the kiss was over, Bernie instinctively pointed his flashlight at the guilty parties. There was a shriek of dismay from Lisa Wondermore, and angry words from Eugene, plus a whole big commotion from all the people around them. "Hey we're trying to watch the movie!" "Turn that thing off!"

Bernie came to his senses, clicked off the flashlight, and hurried toward the safety of the lobby. Thank goodness the terrible incident had lasted only a few seconds, but he knew that his troubles had only just begun.

Bernie nervously tapped his flashlight against his leg, stared at the movie poster for "The Blob" and tried to think of what to do. He realized now that Clark Olsen must be in love with Lisa Wondermore. What he had really been asking Bernie to do was spy on her and Eugene.

Bernie swallowed hard and his face winced as though in pain. He knew the look Clark would get on his face when he told him about the hand-holding and the kiss. He had seen it hundreds of times - anger and scorn - usually directed at himself and Alex. He knew that somehow, some way, even though the kiss was not at all his fault, Clark would blame it on him.

Bernie glanced at his watch. In exactly two and a half hours Clark would be waiting for him. His stomach churning, he ducked back into the theater and clicked on his flashlight, glad to have something to do. He inhaled the wonderful aroma of popcorn and reached down to pick up an empty candy box. But his worry would not go away. Just like the Blob, it continued to grow and grow and grow.

By the end of the second feature, the kiss and Clark Olsen's reaction to it were the only things on Bernie's mind. Even picking up trash, a task he usually found enjoyable, didn't help. As he moved through the theater, Bernie felt the presence of something so real and so sinister, it made him think of a saying that Grandpa had about having a monkey on your back. A couple of times, Bernie wouldn't have been surprised to glance over his shoulder and see the creepy sneering grin of a chimpanzee.

He figured the absolute worst thing Clark could do was

throw him and Alex out of the Blazing Bandits. That would mean all the guys voting them out, which was entirely possible since Clark had always been able to bully, intimidate or charm the other big boys into doing whatever he wanted. Bernie tried not to think of it.

When the movie had been over for half an hour and the theater was clean and Bernie could put it off no longer, he retrieved his coat and hat from behind the snack bar and opened the door to the outside world. There, just as he said he would be, was Clark Olsen, his hands deep in his pockets and a frown on his face. "Well ... you finally decided to show up! What took you so long?"

"Sorry," said Bernie.

The two of them started walking up Lincoln Street. "All right, I want you to tell me everything," said Clark. "And don't leave anything out. I saw them leave the theater. Eugene's mom picked them up in a big fancy Oldsmobile. What a creep. He thinks he's so great. He opened the door for her and everything. I'd like to smack him a good one. How can Lisa even stand to be with him?"

Bernie just shrugged his shoulders and said, "Beats me."

"Okay," said Clark. "So they paid their money and went into the theater. What happened after that? You did watch them, didn't you?"

"I watched 'em," said Bernie. "They stood in line at the snack bar for a long time. Lisa got some Junior Mints and a small root beer. Eugene got an extra large 7 Up and a jumbo box of Good and Plentys."

"That pig," said Clark. "I bet he ate 'em all, too."

"Yep, I think he did," said Bernie.

Clark spit the wad of chewing gum he'd been chomping onto the sidewalk. "Where'd they sit?"

Bernie hesitated. "Um, in the back row."

"The back row!" Clark smacked his fist into his open palm. "The back row! You know what that means. That's like ... lover's lane. Oh man, this is worse than I figured."

Head down, scuffing his feet along the sidewalk, Clark seemed lost in his own private world. Bernie, who had expected things to go a whole lot worse than this, suddenly brightened up. "I saw the previews for 'The Blob.' It looks like it's gonna be really good. You think there could ever be a real thing like the Blob? I mean, here in our town?"

Instead of answering the question, Clark just gave Bernie a mean look and said, "There was probably a whole bunch of em, huh? Sitting in the back row together?"

"Nope," said Bernie. "I'm pretty sure the people around

them were strangers. High school kids, I think."

Clark scuffed his tennis shoes so violently on the sidewalk, you could hear them squeak a block away. Then he confided to Bernie, "I remember when I was in third grade, all us guys used to called Eugene 'Jeannie' on account of that he runs like a girl. He still runs like a girl. I hate him."

"So what else happened?" Clark asked.

"Not much. They were mostly pretty boring. They just talked and ate their candy."

"What did they talk about?" asked Clark. "Did they do anything?"

Bernie pretended not to hear.

Something seemed to snap in Clark then. He stopped walking, squinted his eyes down to pinpoints, peered into Bernie's face and said, "You're holding out on me, aren't you Bern? I can tell. I can tell there's something you're not saying."

Bernie gulped and took a deep breath and decided to come clean. "It was right at the beginning of 'Frances the Talking Mule Joins the Navy.' I was coming up the aisle, and when I looked up at them, I noticed that they were ... holding hands."

Clark stopped walking and his eyes opened wide with amazement. "Are you sure about that? Are you absolutely sure?"

Bernie made his answer as small as possible. "Yes."

Once again Clark smacked his fist into his open palm and hollered, "I hate Eugene McElravy!"

The two boys had just now reached the public swimming pool, where the afternoon swimmers were beginning to leave the building.

"Anything else?" asked Clark.

"Well, yeah, there was one more thing," said Bernie. Just then he spotted some of the boys from his class, Chuckie and Alex and Toby, coming out of the pool. Frantically Bernie waved toward them. "I gotta go," he told Clark. "I just remembered something I gotta tell those guys. I'll see ya later.'"

"I think not," said Clark, his arm held out like a crossing guard. "Not 'til I hear the rest of the story."

This was the moment Bernie had been dreading all afternoon. He wished with all his might that he was any place else on Earth and that he didn't have to tell Clark the bad news he had so far withheld. "Well," Bernie said, "not only did they hold hands. They also kissed."

Bernie then shut his eyes and waited, for what, he did not know. He was pretty sure Clark wouldn't hit him, but he cringed away, just in case. Definitely, he figured, there would be some yelling. Maybe some swearing. It was hard to know. But when there was nothing, no reaction at all, he slowly opened his left eye, then his right eye, and looked at Clark Olsen. What he saw stayed with him for a long, long time. Clark's face, which was usually so quick to furl into a frown or a smart-alecky sneer, looked like someone had taken a dishrag and wiped off every bit of expression. And along with it, the color too.

"I ... I gotta sit down," said Clark. "I feel woozy." They were right by a three-foot brick wall and the grassy green smoothness of someone's freshly mowed lawn. Clark sat down and put his chin on his hands and blinked his eyes about a thousand times. Bernie, courteously, looked the other way. Clark didn't say anything for the longest time; he just stared off toward the waterfront. Bernie started to think, *maybe this isn't going to turn out so bad after all.* He started to wonder what his mother was making for dinner, and what adventures Paladin would have tonight on "Have Gun Will Travel."

Finally Clark said, "They kissed. Right there in the movie theater, they kissed."

Then he jumped up and said, "Well that's just great! That's just peachy! Eugene McElravy is two months younger than me. He doesn't even play basketball. He'll never ever be popular. But Lisa Wondermore would rather go to the movies with him than me!"

Bernie said the first thing he thought of. "Did you ever ask her?"

"Are you crazy?" Clark yelled. "Of course I didn't ask her. You don't ask a girl who's a year older than you are to go to the movies. You just don't. Everyone knows that. I don't know what makes Eugene McElravy think it's okay for him to. Probably because he's such an egomaniac." Clark spat on the sidewalk.

"Egomaniac," said Bernie. "What's that?"

"It's a guy who thinks that everything he does is the best."

Bernie kicked his heels against the bricks for a moment and thought about that. *A guy who thinks everything he does is the best.* That's exactly the way Clark was.

"Well, I'll tell you one thing," said Clark. "She just better forget about me ever asking her anywhere, to do anything, because I'd rather shoot myself in the foot, or jump out of an airplane without a parachute, than have anything to do with her."

Bernie imagined Clark, high up in the sky, in an airplane, unstrapping his parachute, wiping a tear from his eye and jumping out an open door.

"Eugene McElravy! I'll bet his hands were all sweaty! I'll bet his lips were sweaty too!"

"Prob'ly," Bernie agreed. Then he had an unfortunate attack of needing to tell the rest of the story. "When I saw them kissing, I was so surprised, I flashed my flashlight right in their eyes. Eugene started yelling at me. A bunch of other people did too. I got out of there as fast as I could and ran to the lobby."

"What!" yelled Clark. "You caused a major uproar in the theater and you're just now getting around to telling me about it?" He threw his arms up in the air, a huge dramatic gesture, followed by many frowns and looks of disgust.

"Oh great! This is just great! Here I am, sitting on a public street, where everybody in town can see me, and I'm talking to a guy who is so uncool that he shines a flashlight on people during the movie." Clark jumped up. "What if she sees me with you? She'll think I put you up to it. She'll think it was my fault. Thanks a lot, Bern. Thanks a whole lot."

And with that he was gone, stomping up the street. When he was twenty feet away he stopped and shouted over his shoulder, "Someday I'm gonna get you for this!"

When he was thirty feet away he turned around again and added in a voice that was amazingly calm and cool, "Oh and by the way, I just remembered something about that Blob movie. I read that it's based on a true story. It happened in a town pretty much like this one. Right out of nowhere this big green thing rolled into some neighborhood and started gobbling up all the kids. Dogs and cats too."

Bernie gulped and watched Clark as he moved up the street. He knew better than to believe anything Clark Olsen said. He looked over both his shoulders anyway; there was no point in taking chances. Then he jumped off the wall, made a beeline toward Park Street, ran past Clark, and continued running until he was safely at his own front door.

He remembered the joy with which the day had begun and now pondered the enormity of his fear. The world was so big and confusing; you never could tell what was going to happen. It might even be big enough to contain something like the Blob. He opened the door and stepped inside. He could hear his mom and dad talking in the living room, and Charmaine in the kitchen, scolding one of her dolls.

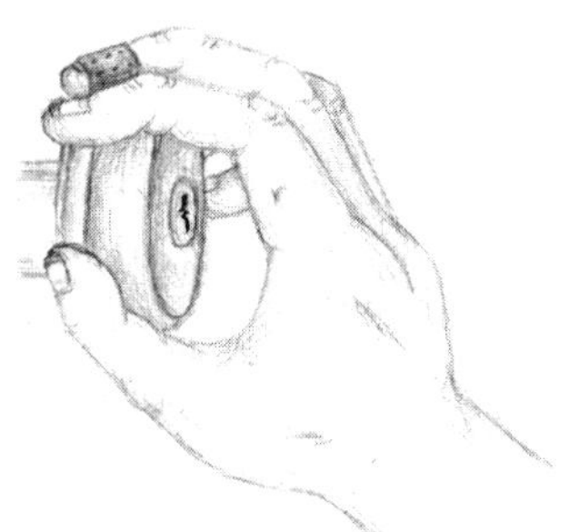

Now things could be good again. Now things could make sense. He was safe. He was home.

Grandpa's Advice

It was a beautiful summer day, not a cloud in the sky, and Bernie Jones was doing his favorite thing. He and Alex were in a part of the neighborhood known as Snake City, creeping as quietly as possible through the tall grass. Already they had caught six red racers. Each time they caught one, they held it up, admired its sleek brown body and thin red stripe, and debated whether or not they had ever caught this particular snake before. Then they turned it loose and watched it slither away in the grass.

They were just about to catch their seventh snake when suddenly Alex reached out and grabbed Bernie by the arm.

"Oh my gosh Bern, I just thought of something. Something really bad." His eyes were wide with the beginnings of panic. In his partially opened mouth was a huge pink wad of chewing gum.

Bernie, who was by nature sympathetic to the feelings of others, especially his best friend, felt his heart sink. "Uh oh," he said. "Did we forget to close the front gate again?" In his mind's eye he saw the Appleby's dog, a Dachshund, running away on his tiny feet and Mrs. Appleby having to drive all the way across town to fetch him from the dog pound ... again.

"Nope, that's not it," said Alex.

"We didn't leave the water running in the basement sink, did we?" The last time they had done that, Mrs. Jones had banished them from the house and they had skulked out of the basement in shame.

"Nope, not that either," said Alex.

"Then what?" Bernie asked.

Almost every day of his life, in some way large or small, he managed to get into some kind of trouble. By now he was so used to it, it didn't really come as a surprise that even a snake hunt could be interrupted by the familiar knot in his stomach that always accompanied trouble.

"I just this minute realized," said Alex, scrunching up his face, "that someday we're gonna grow up."

Bernie stared at his friend in relief and wonder. Alex was capable of saying the most amazing things, totally out of the blue. "Everybody grows up," said Bernie. "So what?"

"So what!" said Alex. "Don't you see? When we're grown up, we'll never ever go on another snake hunt again. We'll be just like our parents. We won't even allow snakes in our house."

Bernie shook his head. "No way. I'll always hunt snakes. I'll never get too old for that."

"Oh yes you will," said Alex, folding his arms across his chest. "You just wait and see."

Bernie sat in silence, trying to imagine a time when he would no longer care about the things he cared about now. His mind flittered through the list of adults he knew and, as hard as he tried, he couldn't think of one who ever caught snakes, or climbed trees, or had contests to see how many marshmallows they could stuff into their mouths. None of them ever played kick the can or capture the flag or even had snowball fights.

"You know something, Alex, you might be right. I never thought about it before, but ... grown-ups hardly ever have any fun." Bernie rocked back on his heels and flopped onto the grass, feeling suddenly hopeless and miserable. "Geez, just when everything was going so good. Why'd you even have to bring it up!" He squinted up at the sky and tried to get back the happy feeling he'd had earlier.

Alex was counting on his fingers all the bad things about being grown up. "We'll have to get jobs, pay rent, wear nice clothes, talk about the weather, take showers all the time."

"But there'll be some good things about being grown up," Bernie said. "We'll be able to drive a car and stay up late and eat as much candy as we want."

"Hmmm, you're right. I hadn't thought about that." Alex tried to imagine the adult version of himself eating a half dozen or so bags of candy. It was a comforting thought, but

it only lasted a few seconds. "You know something, Bern ... I'll bet when we're grown up we won't even care about eating a ton of candy."

This comment caused Bernie to sit upright. "Why not?"

"I don't know," Alex answered honestly. His eyes opened extra wide and he shrugged his shoulders at the unfathomability of it. "You just never see adults eating bags and bags of candy, that's all. I think maybe, when you grow up, your brain goes through some weird change, and stuff like that just doesn't seem important anymore." As he spoke, he nodded his head up and down, lending credibility to the idea.

"That *is* weird," said Bernie, "but I think you might be right."

✲✲✲✲✲✲✲✲✲✲✲

Back at the Jones's house, Bernie's sister Charmaine was at that moment admiring the pink walls and pink ceiling of her bedroom. Reclined on her pink bedspread, an idea suddenly occurred to her, causing her to jump up from her bed and grab her hand mirror. She focused on the face of the girl in the mirror, a girl with round eyeglasses and curly red hair. "Henceforth," she proclaimed, "you shall be called Queen Charmaine." With the mirror she solemnly tapped the tops of her shoulders and added, "May I present Her Royal Highness, Charmaine, Queen of All the World."

From the foot of her bed she grabbed a bath towel, which she pinned around her shoulders, so that it flowed down her back like a velvet cape. She placed her wool hat just so on the top of her head, where it became a crown of diamonds and rubies.

Around and around her room she paraded, to the tune of "March of the May Flowers," which is the song that her musical jewelry box played. Every now and then, when the music box started to slow down, she wound it back up, which made the tiny ballerina inside whirl at a dizzying rate. To enhance her feeling of power, every now and then Charmaine would close the jewelry box, then point her finger at it and say in a stern voice, "Queen Charmaine commands you to dance." When she opened it, the tiny ballerina would whirl around some more, much to the queen's delight.

As she paraded around her room, it occurred to Charmaine that, as queen of the world, she may as well use her royal status against her brother, who hadn't been in trouble for several days. A moment later she was seated at her desk, pink pencil in hand, ready to start a royal list. Charmaine loved making lists. She tapped the pencil against her teeth. "Let's see," she said in a snooty voice, "what is it that bothers the queen most about that horrid peasant boy, Bernie?"

****

In Snake City, as the sun beat down and the maple trees fluttered ever so slightly in the breeze, Bernie and Alex sat in silence, worrying about their future. Two more red racers slithered by. Either boy could have reached out and caught them, but neither of them even bothered to try.

"We *could* ask our moms and dads to tell us about being grown up," said Alex, "except they'd just tell us not to worry. But if you think about it, Bern, how many times have you ever seen your parents having fun? I mean, the kind of fun that really *is* fun? Not just standing around yacking with other grown-ups."

Bernie took a moment to mull the question over, propping his hand under his chin and narrowing the focus of his gaze onto one particular blade of grass. Last year on their summer vacation, when his parents had rented a bicycle built for two, they had laughed and giggled the whole time. Once he had seen his mother playing with Charmaine's hula hoop. But what did his parents do for fun the rest of the time? It seemed like mostly they just worked and read the newspaper and talked about grown-up stuff. Things a kid would never waste their time on.

Bernie crossed and uncrossed his eyes, making the single blade of grass two, then one, then two, then one. With no plan for doing so, suddenly he plucked the blade of grass, stretched it tight between his thumbs and blew out a high-pitched screeching sound, which inspired Alex to do the same thing. In the next moment they were rolling around, trying to stuff handfuls of grass down each other's shirt. When they stopped to catch their breath, Alex stared off at the sky and said, "Yessirree, it's gonna be a real shame when we have to grow up and stop having fun."

Bernie's spirits took an immediate nosedive. But instead of sulking, he jumped to his feet and said, "I know! Let's go down to the senior center and talk to my grandpa about it.

He always helps me figure stuff out."

"Good idea!" said Alex, and the two boys instantly took their leave of Snake City.

The senior center was only five blocks away. Augustus Jones had a private room with a bed and two easy chairs, a TV, a tiny kitchen and a great big window that looked out onto Park Street. Bernie was allowed, any time he wanted, to walk to the senior center and visit Grandpa.

As Bernie and Alex made their way down Park Street, each boy, without thinking about it, found a rock to kick along the sidewalk. It helped to distract them from the seriousness of their thoughts, and before they knew it, they had reached their destination.

They found Grandpa Jones sitting in the parlor, listening to a silver-haired lady play the piano. Grandpa's eyes were closed and there was a big smile on his face. He was thinking about a time long ago, about his first automobile, and the first girl he ever took for a ride in it. In the next instant his thoughts were interrupted by a familiar voice.

"Grandpa! Grandpa! We need to ask you something!"

Alex and Bernie were both talking at once, which interrupted the piano player, who turned around and scowled at them. Grandpa smiled at her in apology and suggested to the boys that they walk down the hall to his room; obviously they had something serious on their minds.

Bernie started the story. “We were down in Snake City. We’d just caught six snakes ...”

Alex chimed in, “We were just about ready to catch number seven ...”

“When all of a sudden,” Bernie continued, “Alex realized that someday we’ll be grown up! And that when that happens, we’ll never have any more fun. We’ll just have jobs to go to and bills to pay and problems all the time.” He shrugged his shoulders and held the palms of his hands up to show what a hopeless situation it was.

“We don’t want that to happen,” said Alex, “so we came to you for advice.”

“Hmmm,” said Grandpa. “This is a serious subject.” He stood up and went to stare out his window, which is what he always did when he needed a few minutes to think. When he turned to face the boys, he asked them, “How much time do you boys figure you’ve got?”

Bernie and Alex stared at each other with blank expressions until finally Bernie said, "Well, we're both ten years old, so we've got maybe three, four, five years. Not a lot of time."

"Yeah," said Alex. "By the time we're thirteen we'll probably start taking showers every day and wearing clean clothes all the time. We might even have girlfriends!"

"No way!" said Bernie. "I'm never having a girlfriend. *Or* taking a shower every day!"

"Well, me neither," said Alex. "But you never know. We could change our minds. That's exactly what happened to my brother Kevin. He used to be just a regular kid. Now he takes a shower and wears good clothes every day."

Bernie shook his head in disgust. He too had watched Kevin, almost overnight, go from being a normal, ordinary guy to a cleaned up, spiffed up teenager whose favorite thing to do was talk on the phone with girls. The thought of it made Bernie panic. Is that really what would happen to him and Alex? Couldn't anything be done?

"Hold on a minute, boys," Grandpa said. "I think I might be able to help you. How about we go for a little walk into town? There's something I want to show you." He took off his bedroom slippers and put on his shoes, then his coat and hat.

Grandpa was the last to leave the room. He fixed a serious gaze on the man in the mirror and said to himself, "Augustus, you've got a mighty big responsibility here. These boys are counting on you. So you'd better think of something, and you'd better think of it fast!"

Bernie had not yet been told, but his parents had been having a bit of a problem with Grandpa lately. When you live at the senior center, you aren't supposed to just put on your coat and hat and walk out the door any time you want. You are supposed to check out at the front desk, tell them exactly where you're going and when you're coming back. But Grandpa said he thought that was all a bunch of hooey and, whenever he felt like it, he just slipped out the back door. Which is exactly what he and Bernie and Alex did now.

"Ah, that sunshine feels good!" he said as soon as they were outside. " Now let's just go see if we can find a solution to your problem."

❊❊❊❊❊❊❊❊❊❊❊

In her best handwriting, Queen Charmaine compiled a list of offenses committed by the peasant boy who lived in her castle. In big curlicue letters at the top of the page, she had written, "Things Bernie Does That Drive Me Crazy." Number one was "whistles through his teeth." Number two: "cracks his knuckles." Three: "wolfs down his food." Four: "loves bugs and snakes." Five: "listens to cowboy music." Six: "tries to yodel." Seven: "breathes too loud."

She could have gone on and on, but at that moment she heard the family's station wagon pull up in the driveway. Her mother was returning home from the grocery store. She picked up her hand mirror and said to the queen, "Methinks it is high time the sheriff of the Jones Kingdom should be informed of Her Royal Highness's discontent." Charmaine grabbed her list and started for the kitchen.

As Bernie and Alex and Grandpa made their way down Park Street toward town, they discovered lots of big mud puddles to walk through. Instead of going around them, Grandpa walked right through the puddles too. A couple of them he even jumped in, laughing as the mud splattered on Bernie and Alex.

They had only gone a short distance when Grandpa suggested they stop for ice cream cones, which was good, because Alex and Bernie were starting to get hungry. After that, they walked along the waterfront and watched the ships come in and out of the harbor.

"I think I'll take my shoes off and run my tootsies through the sand," Grandpa said, plopping himself down and pulling off his shoes and socks. "I always say, there's nothing like letting your feet loose in the sand. But ..." his voice grew serious, "you have to keep a close eye on them because you never know ... they might just run away!"

Bernie and Alex took their shoes off too, and pretty soon all three were kicking sand at each other and running in the shallow surf. After a while they rolled up their pant legs and, even though the water was cold, went wading up to their knees.

Grandpa was the first one out. He said he felt like building a sand fort. The two boys volunteered to help him and pretty soon they had an elaborate castle with moats and a rock wall all around for protection.

After a while Grandpa said, “I don’t know about you boys, but that ice cream didn’t really fill me up. I think I need a hot dog. Maybe two. Maybe three. What do you say?”

The boys jumped up and they all took off for the snack bar. “Have as many as you want, but just one at a time,” Grandpa said. With that he turned to the man behind the counter. “Make mine a jumbo dog with relish, ketchup and mustard. Lots and lots of mustard. And give these boys whatever they want.”

Bernie could only eat two hot dogs, although he had hoped to eat four. Alex couldn’t quite finish his second, so he wrapped it up in a napkin and put it in his pocket for later.

That’s when they remembered why they were on this outing in the first place. Bernie took a long slurpy sip of his root beer and said, “So tell us Grandpa, what’s it like to be a grown-up? Is it really as bad as it seems?”

Grandpa stared out at the water. “Well, Bernie, like most things, it has its good points and it has its bad points. Now on the good side, as you might already have considered, you can eat whatever you like, whenever you like. Cookies, candy, hot dogs, hamburgers, pizza, tacos, chips, you name it. Plus you can stay up ‘til midnight every night of the week if you want. You can go to the movies most any time. You can pretty much do anything, so long as it’s legal and you've got the money."

"I'd sure like to stay up 'til midnight anytime I wanted." Alex said.

Bernie agreed. "Yeah. If I was a grown-up, I'd never go to bed."

"The only problem with that," Grandpa said, "is that it might make you late for work in the morning. If you're late for work, you might lose your job."

Bernie asked, "Will we have to have jobs, Grandpa?"

"Yep. If you want to have money, you've got to have a job, that's just the way it goes. But look at it this way, boys. You could be firemen, or race car drivers, or deep sea divers, or astronauts. Not all jobs mean you have to wear a suit and tie, or work inside."

"But what about having fun, Grandpa?" said Bernie. "When we grow up, does that mean we have to stop having fun? And will we start thinking that bugs and worms and snakes are creepy? Because if that's what it means, I don't think I can stand to grow up!"

Instead of answering, Grandpa jumped up and said, "Follow me, boys. I've got something to show you."

There was a trail that lead from the waterfront back toward town. It was one that the big boys sometimes talked about, but Bernie and Alex had never used before. "This path has been here a long time," said Grandpa. "Back when I was a boy, we always used this trail. Not too many people do nowadays, though. As you can see, the grass is tall, which makes it hard to walk. Plus there's another reason most people don't like this trail."

"What's that, Grandpa?"

Before Grandpa could answer, Bernie looked down, and there at his feet, he saw for himself: snakes, just like in his own back yard. There were more snakes than any boy could ever hope to catch.

"On your mark, get set, go!" said Grandpa. "Last guy to

catch one is a rotten egg!" For the next hour the three of them caught one snake after another, compared each one, showed them off with pride, then turned them loose in the tall grass.

✻✻✻✻✻✻✻✻✻✻✻

In the quiet of the Jones's kitchen, Queen Charmaine tried to figure out the best place to leave her list. Her parents, of course, were already familiar with her many complaints about Bernie. But maybe, she thought, if they saw, in black and white, just how many bad habits Bernie really *did* have, they would be inspired to, once and for all, make him straighten up and fly right.

Charmaine scanned the room, looking for the best place to leave her list. She settled on the spot at the back of the kitchen sink, right next to the dish soap. Her mother spent plenty of time at the sink; she was bound to see it there. Charmaine pushed one of the chairs over from the table and climbed on. She propped the list up just so, and started to climb back down. Instead of thinking about what she was doing, she was imagining what the new, improved Bernie would be like (once their parents started cracking down on him). That's when her foot slipped off the chair and she smacked her chin on the edge of the sink. BLOOD! Oh my goodness, there was blood! The queen was unhappy! The queen was in pain! Her parents were in the back yard, so out the door she ran, screaming bloody murder all the way.

It turned out that Charmaine's wound was minor and hardly even painful after a few minutes, which, after all that blood, and knowing Bernie would call her clumsy, really made her mad. She spent the rest of the day on the couch, with an ice pack on her chin, suffering. To her way of thinking, the whole thing was Bernie's fault, because if it hadn't been for his bad habits, she wouldn't have been climbing on the chair in the first place.

When Mrs. Jones found Charmaine's list, she gave it a quick glance, had a good laugh, then tossed it in the trash. "That girl," she said to herself, "what will she think of next?"

****

Bernie, Alex and Grandpa turned all the snakes loose, then the three of them headed back to the senior center. The boys were surprised when Grandpa suddenly stopped and pulled a beautiful little red racer out of his shirt pocket, holding it up for the boys to admire.

"What're you going to do with it?" they asked.

"Oh there's a certain nurse, Mrs. McGillicutty, who always gives me a hard time. I can't wait to see what she does when I show her this!" A devilish smile spread across Grandpa's face as he tucked the snake back into his pocket.

A few minutes later the three of them were back at the senior center, where Grandpa waved them good-bye. Bernie and Alex started the walk back up Park Street.

Alex pulled the remains of his hot dog out of his pocket and crammed a huge bite into his mouth. Bits of it flew from his mouth as he spoke. "Feel any better now that we've talked to your grandpa, Bern?"

"I guess so," Bernie said, "because even though we still have to grow up someday and get jobs and all that, maybe we'll be able to figure out a way to have some fun every now and then. Grandpa is eighty-two and it sure seemed like he was having fun today."

Just then they heard the sound of a woman's voice from inside the senior center, screaming at the top of her lungs.

"Yeah," Alex said, stuffing the last of the hot dog into his mouth. "Maybe it won't be so bad after all."

Crisis on Peabody Creek

Bernie tightened up the laces on his tennis shoes, jostled his backpack around ‘til it rested just so on his shoulders, and was off to meet up with Joey Wondermore and Alex. The three boys had gotten permission from their parents, to pack a lunch and hike along Peabody Creek, all the way to town. It was only a mile and a half, but it was pretty rough going. They’d never been allowed to make the trip before, but since Joey was twelve, all the parents finally agreed it was okay. Bernie squinted up at the sky, and he knew beyond a doubt ... this was going to be a day he’d never forget.

In front of Appleby’s house Alex was bouncing his basketball, staring down at the sidewalk, concentrating on getting the ball to bounce to precisely the same height each time. When he saw Bernie he tossed the ball over his shoulder into the yard and ambled down the street.

Bernie greeted him with a huge smile. “Great day for a hike, huh?”

“Yeah, I guess so,” said Alex, who had a secret fear about the day’s adventure.

“I wish we were hiking a whole lot farther,” said Bernie. “A mile and a half, that’s not far. We could do that in our sleep.”

Alex scrunched his mouth up. “Uhmmm, there’s somethin’ I gotta ask you Bern. Do you think there might be any bobcats or cougars in the woods?”

”Nnnnn I don’t think so,” said Bernie. “But maybe we’ll get lucky and see one.”

Alex, who knew Bernie was not making fun of him, said, “Yeah, maybe we’ll get to see one. That’d be great.”

And just then, there was Joey Wondermore, rounding the corner, swinging his lunch bag.

Joey was a slender, tall boy with sandy brown hair and an inquisitive mind. A bookworm by nature, he was more of an indoor person than an outdoor person. Having spent a bit of time with Bernie and Alex, however, had taught him that there was much more to appreciate in nature than he had so far realized. Snakes, for instance: what interesting creatures they were.

The boys cut through the brush that lead down into Peabody

Gulch and were soon out of sight of their houses. At the bottom of the trail was a little beach where they'd always been allowed to wade, but the upper and lower stretches of Peabody Creek had been off limits before.

They took off their shoes, rolled up the bottoms of their pant legs and prepared to take their first steps into the creek. Brrr! Cold! As they walked along, Joey took the lead and Bernie brought up the rear. This left Alex in the middle, where he felt most safe, and as they ventured into new territory, he started staring hard at every tree trunk and clump of bushes, to make sure there were no animals lurking. Soon the creek bed would be too hard to follow, and they'd have to veer up into the woods. Alex had read that if you were in the woods and there were wild animals around, it was smart to make a lot of noise.

"Hey Joey," he said, kind of offhandedly, trying to make it seem as though he was just now thinking it up, "remember when you told us how much you like telling stories. Feel like telling us one right now?"

Joey had picked up a willow branch, which he used as a walking stick. He swished it into the tall grass, thought about it for a second, and said, "Well ... I could tell you guys the story of Ernest Shackleton. He was an Antarctic explorer."

"Ernest Shackleton?" said Bernie. "I've never heard of him."

"He was from Ireland," said Joey. "On one expedition he

and a bunch of other guys went down to Antarctica, to try and be the first ones ever to cross the continent. But before they got there, their ship got stuck in the middle of the ice, and they ended up drifting around in it for ten whole months."

"Wow," said Bernie. "That's almost a year. Couldn't they get unstuck?"

"Nope," said Joey, whacking clumps of grass. "Once you're in the middle of the Antarctic Ocean and the ice starts to close in on you, you're going wherever it's going."

"What was the name of their ship?" asked Alex.

"It was called the *Endurance*," said Joey. "And that's a pretty good name for it too, because of all the stuff they had to go through."

The boys stopped to have a drink from their canteens and admire this stretch of the creek, so near their neighborhood, yet so far away.

"Like ... what kind of stuff did they have to go through?" asked Bernie.

Joey squinted his eyes against the sun, took a long drink of cherry kool-aid and said, "Eventually the ice squeezed the ship so tight, it crushed it. Just squished it like a bug. After that they lived in their tents on the ice."

"For how long?" asked Alex.

"Mmm, about six months."

Alex shivered, even though he wasn't the least bit cold. "How'd they ever get warm?"

"They didn't," said Joey, "at least not for very long. They were always wet and cold. Plus all around them the ice was cracking and breaking off, huge big chunks, so it was dangerous just being there at all."

The three boys had reached a part of the creek where the lower limbs of some of the maple trees extended quite a way out into the water. In some places they could step over them, but finally they had to climb the bank and search for the trail through the woods.

Alex immediately grew uncomfortable. Because his parents owned the local theater, he'd seen the movie "Demon Versus Dracula" six times, and the demon had been a bobcat, a wild, screaming creature with fangs and claws the size of butcher knives. Clark Olsen and the other big boys had started a rumor that a similar kind of wildcat lived down in Peabody Gulch.

Ordinarily, Alex would just laugh at such a dumb idea, but now that they were here, deep down in the ravine, even just an ordinary bobcat, or a cougar, which occasionally *did* come down from the mountains, was more than he wanted to see.

So he started singing, "A horse is a horse of course of course, and no one can talk to a horse of course ..." So intent was

Alex on making noise, lots of loud noise, that he walked right into the back of Joey Wondermore, who had come to a standstill in front of him.

"I hate that song!" said Joey. "Every time I hear it, it gets stuck in my head and it won't go away!"

"Sorry," said Alex. "I hate it too, but ... I just felt like singing."

"I want to hear about what happened to Ernest Shackleton and all those guys after they left their ship," said Bernie.

Joey turned around and started picking a path through the bushes and trees.

"Well, there were lots of seals around, so that's mainly what they ate. They took all the stuff they needed off the ship, including their three lifeboats, and just drifted with the ice pack for another six or seven months until they got to open water. Then they launched their boats."

"Where did they go then?" asked Bernie, with a note of worry in his voice.

Joey whacked at another clump of bushes. "By day the men rowed their lifeboats, and at night they'd stop and camp on an iceberg. Eventually they came to a place called Elephant Island."

"How come it was called that?" asked Alex. "Were there elephants there?"

Joey laughed. "Elephants! No way! Antarctica is down at the bottom of the world, where it's colder and windier than any place on Earth. You'd never find an elephant there."

"Yeah? Well sometimes," Alex said, scanning every bush, every tree trunk, every clump of grass, "animals show up where you don't expect them to."

Bernie and Joey exchanged confused looks. Neither of them was worried about what might be lurking in the woods, so they didn't understood what Alex was really saying.

"Yeah, well, there were no elephants on this island," said Joey. "There wasn't anything there. And some of those guys, well ... they were in kind of bad shape. You know, being out in the cold all the time, and not having the right kinds of stuff to eat. That can be really bad for you. Shackleton knew they couldn't make it through another winter, so he did the most amazing thing."

And right then Joey Wondermore did the most amazing thing. The boys had reached a clearing, where Joey knelt down, unstrapped his backpack, reached inside and pulled out ... a boomerang. Neither Bernie or Alex had ever seen one up close before. "Watch your heads!" Joey shouted, then he threw the thing with a snap of his wrist. It flew out and arched around and then, miraculously, headed back straight toward them. Bernie and Alex, both delighted and stupefied, ducked just as Joey caught the boomerang. Though he tried not to smile, a look of triumph spread across his face.

"Wow! Where'd you get that?" the boys asked. They wanted to learn how to throw it too.

Joey showed them a few tricks. Mostly they ended up flinging it into the brush and having to go search for it. Alex made a point of throwing it without much gusto so he wouldn't have to hunt around in the bushes. But still it was fun. They messed around with the boomerang so long, they all got hungry, so they found a good spot for lunch and started gobbling down all the food they had packed.

"Maybe we should save some of this food," suggested Joey. "We might get hungry later on."

"Nah, I'm starved," said Bernie, who loved eating out of doors.

"Yeah, we can get an ice cream cone when we get to town,"

said Alex.

“We’d better get going if we’re gonna get there before the Big Scoop closes,” said Joey, checking his watch. “A mile and a half might not sound like that much, but when it’s along a creek like this, and part of it’s in the woods, it takes a lot longer than you might think.”

They all got up and started for the trail. “Want me to tell you what Shackleton did next?” he asked.

“Yeah,” said Alex, looking over his shoulders again, at the dark shadowy shapes all around him. “And talk loud because it’s kinda hard to hear when we’re walking.”

“Well,” said Joey, “Ernest Shackleton was a man of action. He saw that something had to be done right away and he did it. He took one of the lifeboats and five of the men, and they sailed eight hundred miles through one of the most dangerous stretches of water in the world - in a boat that was only twenty-five feet long.”

“That’s not very big!” said Alex, whose father owned a twenty-foot fishing boat.

“Eight hundred miles,” Bernie said. “That’s a long way!”

Already, on their own brief hike, the sun had traveled part way across the sky. What would it be like, to travel eight hundred miles in a small boat, in the roughest water in the world? For a while everyone seemed to be lost in their own thoughts, and they trudged along in silence.

With the sun in his eyes, and his mind on other things, Joey failed to notice a tree limb which caught on his shoelace, causing him to fall. His pain was immediate, a sharp pain in his ankle. He bit his lip to keep from crying; he'd only been friends with these guys for a couple months, and no way did he want them to see him cry. But it hurt! Oh how it hurt!

He danced around on his good foot for a minute, trying to somehow make the pain go away, then he crumpled to the ground.

"Are you all right? Are you okay?" Bernie and Alex both asked.

"Yeah, I'm okay," he said, after a few seconds, "but ... one of you guys has gotta go get some help. I can't walk."

These words brought instant terror to Alex. He could think of nothing worse than being in the woods alone.

"I'll go," said Bernie. "Town can't be too far away. I'll just follow the creek."

He and Alex helped Joey to a rock where he could sit and soak his ankle in the cool water.

"You guys stay right here," said Bernie. "I'll be back as soon as I can."

Joey groaned, "Just hurry up and get going." And with that, Bernie took off.

****

He wasn't worried at first, because he figured he was pretty close to town, but then the creek just kept going and going and going, twisting and turning, turning and twisting. He wished now they hadn't eaten all the food because it might be a while before he could get back. Those guys would be hungry. By then it might even be dark, so they'd be cold too.

On his trek, alone, with his mind flitting from one thing to another, it suddenly dawned on Bernie that Alex was afraid that a wild animal might come down from the mountains and attack him. Bernie didn't even have to think about it; he knew it for an absolute fact. It was silly, of course, but Bernie knew all about silly fears. He had one himself, that he didn't want anyone to know about ... he couldn't stand the sight of blood. Especially his own.

Bernie had left the creek - there were too many branches to climb over - and was trying to follow the trail through the woods, when he noticed that the sun had vanished behind a lot of dark clouds, and it was starting to get windy. Oh great! Just what he didn't need. Occupied with these thoughts, he too, caught his foot on the limb of a tree, and down he went, crashing through many layers of limbs. Ouch! Pain! He was pretty sure it wasn't serious, only scrapes, but there was blood everywhere, on his knees, on his arms; he even had a cut on his forehead. The sight of all that blood, rolling down his arms and legs and into his eyes made him woozy. He had to stop and tell himself, *it's all right, it's okay.* But the other thought he had - the stronger thought - was *oh boy, we're really in trouble now.*

Back at the creek, Joey and Alex were confident that Bernie was taking care of things, so they relaxed and talked, and Joey showed Alex the boomerang again. But after a while Joey, because he was by nature a quiet boy, and also because he was in pain, withdrew into himself, and just stared at the creek in silence.

The quiet, along with the gathering storm clouds, unnerved Alex. As long as the two of them were talking or laughing, he was fine. But with all the silence, his worrying started up again. He hated bothering Joey, he knew his ankle hurt, but Alex just had to start singing again, "A horse is a horse of course of course ..." On and on he sang: the song from "*Rawhide*," the "*Mickey Mouse Club Theme*," anything he could think of. When he didn't stop, Joey finally had to put his fingers in his ears, to make the terrible noise go away. Alex took this as a signal that he could continue to sing to his heart's content, so he did. His favorite song, "*Ninety-Nine Bottles of Beer on the Wall*," worked so well, he sang it all the way through three times in a row.

****

When the storm clouds broke, and rain poured from the sky, Bernie had been standing in the same spot for five full minutes, bawling his eyes out, feeling terribly sorry for himself. Not only was he all alone and cut and bleeding, now he was drenched clear through and the wind was whipping the branches of all the maple trees into a ghostly, eerie sound. More than anything, Bernie wished he could be somewhere where there were people, and that he was warm and drinking cocoa, and that there weren't all these scary sounds.

He thought about how, when he was a little kid and he got hurt and cried, somebody always came and helped him. But today, no matter how much he cried, that was not going to happen. Whatever *did* happen was completely up to him. So he wiped away his tears and blood and found a big stump to lean on. Then he asked himself, *what would Ernest Shackleton do in a situation like this?* Joey had said that he was a man of action, so obviously, if he was in a jam like this, he would just keep on going. He would bring back help. With that in mind, Bernie stood up, took a deep breath, put one foot in front of the other, and marched toward his destination.

****

When it started raining, Alex and Joey left the creek bed and headed for the woods, seeking shelter among the trees. Alex hadn't wanted to; he told Joey they should stay where they were. But since he didn't want to tell him the reason why, Joey, the older of the two, had limped to the shelter of a big maple tree, which they now sat under, shivering in their wet tee shirts.

Alex could tell that Joey was annoyed with him, so he said, "I promise I'll stop singing, but you've gotta tell me some more of the Shackleton story, okay? And you gotta tell it to me real loud, 'cause with the wind and everything, it's kinda hard to hear." When Joey gave him a puzzled look, Alex thumped the side of his head a couple times and added, "I also think there's a chance I might be going deaf. I think it runs in our family."

Joey was just glad to be out of the rain. "Well, first of all," he told Alex, "when you're in a twenty-five foot boat in the water around Antarctica, you're in a desperate situation. If the boat swamps, that's it. That's all she wrote." He drew his index finger across his throat, to demonstrate just how desperate the situation was.

"For sixteen days Shackleton and the five other men sailed and rowed through the stormiest water in the world. Their destination was South Georgia Island, where there was a whaling station. But since they had to navigate by dead reckoning, there was only about one chance in a jillion that they could find it. They were drenched and frozen and starving. There was no reason for them to think they could survive."

Joey shook his head and gave Alex a solemn look, as though bad news was on the way. Then he broke into a smile.

"Just when things looked their worst, good old Shackleton pulled it out of the bag and they got there; they actually made it to South Georgia Island. But the whaling station was on the other side of the island. In order to get there, they had to cross a whole mountain range, which no one had ever climbed before."

"That's not fair," said Alex. "After everything those guys had to go through, and now they've gotta climb a mountain. I guess, they're probably doomed, huh?"

"Kinda looks that way, doesn't it?" said Joey. "But, actually, this story has a happy ending."

"It does?" said Alex. "What happens?"

While Joey told the next chapter of the tale, half a mile downstream, Bernie was slogging his way through the water and bushes, shivering, cold, wet and hungry. Every time he came to a new twist or turn of the creek, he figured, *I'll be able to see town around the next bend.* But it was always the same: more trees, more rocks, more branches to step over, and town was nowhere in sight. The creek seemed to be endless. The sky was getting darker, and he was getting tired. Finally, when Bernie was just about certain he couldn't go any farther, he rounded another bend in the creek, and there, up ahead, he could see the harbor and the main street that lead into town. A few hundred more yards and he heard the honking of horns and the rush of traffic. Soon he was in the midst of it.

Wet, tired, thirsty and hungry, Bernie raked his fingers through his hair, opened the door of Neibert Brothers gas station and asked if he could use the phone. He almost cried with relief when he heard his mother's voice.

Fifteen minutes later Mr. and Mrs. Jones were at the gas station with food and flashlights and extra jackets. Bernie could tell, his mother was alarmed when she saw him. He had thought about getting some paper towels and cleaning himself up while he waited for his parents, but instead he just inspected his cuts and bruises, amazed at how many of them there were.

Bernie and his parents drove to the spot where Peabody Creek enters the harbor and started the hike back in. By then the rain had stopped and the sky was clearing a little, and the gulley didn't seem at all treacherous or scary, the way it had earlier. With his dad in the lead and Bernie in the middle, he felt completely rejuvenated. Now that he actually *was* rescuing his friends, he felt like he could hike this creek bed forever.

****

It only took them an hour to reach Joey and Alex, who had moved from their spot in the woods back out by the creek. Joey was giving Alex another lesson in how to throw the boomerang and everything seemed under control.

Still, the boys were overjoyed to see their rescuers, and Alex came running, to greet his best friend. When he saw all of Bernie's scrapes and cuts, he stepped back and asked, "What happened to you, Bern?"

Bernie beamed with pride. "I had a little trouble along the way," he said, "but nothing I couldn't handle."

While Mr. Jones examined Joey's ankle, Bernie thought to ask, "By the way, Joey, I was wondering ... did Shackleton make it back okay? Did he bring some help?"

"Yyyyip," said Joey. "He had to scale a mountain first, but eventually he reached a whaling station and got some help and went back and rescued every last man. He didn't lose a single one."

"Wow," said Bernie. "Twenty-six guys and all of 'em pulled through."

It was time to pack everything up and head back to town. They all started, single-file down the trail, with Mr. Jones in the rear, piggybacking Joey. Just as the last bit of sun sank from the sky, they reached the car, and their long day of adventuring on Peabody Creek came to an end.

By the time Bernie got to bed, he was so tired, he started dreaming before he even closed his eyes. When his mother came in to kiss him good night, he told her, "I'm never ever gonna forget that story. All that ice. Elephant Island. That little boat. Climbing a mountain. And he didn't lose a single guy!"

Bernie closed his eyes and immediately felt himself floating away. His bed was a tiny boat, he was adrift on a stormy sea, but there was a full moon overhead and stars were twinkling in the sky, and Bernie Jones was not at all afraid.

The Penny Hike

Bernie sat on Alex's front steps, his elbow resting on his knee, his chin resting on his hand, waiting for Alex to come out and play. Alex had been at his cousin's house for almost a week, and Bernie couldn't wait to see him. A week is a long time not to see your best friend.

As he stared off into space, Bernie's thoughts drifted to the new bike he was planning to buy. He'd been saving up his allowance and birthday money for a long time, and soon he'd be zooming all over the neighborhood; it was a ten-speed, after all.

Then the door opened and Alex appeared. "Bern! You should've come in. The door was open. How ya doin'? What'd I miss while I was gone?"

A big smile spread across Bernie's face and he thought,

good old Alex.

"I can't believe I've been gone a whole week. I've got so much stuff to tell you. What'dya feel like doin'?"

"I don't care," said Bernie. "What do *you* feel like doing?"

"Hmm." Alex stared toward the Patterson's tetherball pole with a serious look on his face, biting his lower lip in concentration. "How about we go on a penny hike?"

"A penny hike," said Bernie. "What's that?"

"It's where we go on a hike, only we don't know where we're going."

"Sounds good to me," said Bernie. He started to stand, got halfway up, then turned to ask Alex, "But if we don't know where we're going, how will we know where to go?"

"Simple," said Alex, as he pushed his thick eyeglasses back onto the bridge of his nose. "We start off on the street corner and take turns. When it's my turn I point one way and say, 'Heads it's this way,' then I point another way and say, 'tails it's that way.' Then I flip a coin and whatever comes up, we walk that way for one block. Then it's your turn. You pick a direction for heads and one for tails, flip the coin and the penny tells us which way to go."

"I get it," said Bernie. "That's why they call it a penny hike."

"Yup," said Alex, proud to once again be the bringer of new and interesting stuff to the neighborhood. Visits to his cousins in the city often netted these results.

Usually on Saturdays the boys did a variety of things, but no matter whatever else they did, they almost always walked the eight blocks to downtown, where they visited their favorite places: the Big Scoop, Brown's Hardware, the 88-cent store, and any other shops that caught their fancy.

The boys checked with their mothers, grabbed their jackets and met outside, under the apple tree. Like always, they walked to the corner, but instead of turning left and walking toward town, the first flip of the coin sent the boys in the opposite direction, up the hill toward their school. Their next turn took them another block up the hill. Soon they were even farther away from town, so that Bernie had to face the sad fact that, if they played this game long enough, they might never make it to the Big Scoop or Brown's Hardware.

The hardware store had special meaning for Bernie, as it was the home of the shiny black ten-speed Schwinn he hoped to one day own. He had been visiting the bike at least once a week for almost six months now, and in his mind he rode it day and night, around and around and around the neighborhood, up the hill to school and all around town. He figured if he kept saving his allowance and all his birthday money, maybe it would be his by the end of summer. Because Alex was gone last Saturday, Bernie hadn't gone to town, and now it was beginning to look like he wouldn't be going this Saturday either.

With all his heart, Bernie wished he was at the Super Scoop right now, biting into a chocolate fudge cone. He opened his mouth to tell his friend, but at that exact moment Alex said, "Just think Bern, if our moms let us, and we didn't have to go to school, we could go on a penny hike for weeks at a time and maybe end up in a whole different town." Then he stopped dead in his tracks, grabbed Bernie by his shirt sleeve and, with eyes magnified to twice their size by his Coke-bottle eyeglasses said, "We could get in the Guinness Book of World Records!"

Bernie's shoulders positively slumped at the idea of a world-record penny hike. That's when Alex said, "Hey! What are we doing! It's Saturday! We should be downtown."

"That's kind of what I was thinking," said Bernie.

"We could be at the Big Scoop right now," said Alex, who had a sudden, intense desire for an ice cream cone.

Bernie's smile filled up his face. "All right!"

While the boys hurried toward the waterfront, Alex demonstrated another new skill he had acquired while visiting his cousins. He pointed at an approaching car and said, authoritatively, "Buick." The next car he pointed to proudly and said, "Oldsmobile."

As they walked toward town, Alex explained the basics of car identification to Bernie: their overall shape and lines, their hood ornaments and bumpers. "Cadillac. Chevrolet. Ford. Pontiac," Alex said in quick succession, pointing at each oncoming car. In every case he was right, and he was able to convey his knowledge to Bernie, a quick learner in critical matters such as this.

"Okay, next one's mine," Bernie said, and both boys watched a car several blocks away turn toward them. Bernie strained to see the hood ornament and knew, without a doubt. "Ford!"

"Yup," said Alex.

"Wow," said Bernie, who felt suddenly powerful with the learning of this new thing.

Then Bernie's gaze drifted slightly, across the street, and he noticed a woman wearing a blue hat. She looked about Grandpa's age. He had seen her, a few minutes ago, coming out of Myerson's Jewelry. She had walked to the corner, but instead of crossing the street, she had turned around and gone back into the jewelry store. A minute later she stepped back out, headed in the other direction, and disappeared around the corner. Now here she was again, back at the jewelry store.

Alex, staring in the opposite direction, pointed to a shiny yellow and white car and said "Pontiac." He took another lick of his triple-scoop Neapolitan cone, pointed again and said, "Studebaker." Bernie, eager to show off, identified two more Fords, all the while keeping an eye on the blue-hatted lady.

She was going from shop to shop, walking in, then walking right back out. After a while, Bernie could see that something was definitely wrong.

"Look at that lady over there, the one in the blue hat," he said to Alex. "I think there's something wrong with her."

Just as Bernie pointed her out, she settled herself onto the wrought-iron bench by Blaine's Fashion Wear, shaded her eyes with her hand, and began to weep.

"Holy cow," said Bernie, "she's crying."

"Wow," said Alex, straightening up in his seat and taking a lick of his cone. "Maybe she just saw something in one of the stores, and she wants to buy it real bad, but she doesn't have enough money."

"Maybe," said Bernie. "But I don't think so. I've been watching her and something tells me it's not that."

"What could it be then?"

"I don't know," said Bernie. "Maybe her husband just died."

"You think?"

Bernie shrugged his shoulders. "Maybe her husband died and she was having his watch repaired, and the jewelry man accidentally broke it, and now she doesn't have anything left to remind her of him."

Alex just stared at Bernie, kind of confused, his head tilted to the side, which he needed to do anyway, in order to lick the next crucial part of his ice cream cone.

"Well, I'm going over there," said Bernie, standing up.

"You're doing what?" asked Alex.

But Bernie was already crossing the street and approaching the old lady. Alex took several more licks from his cone, squinting into the sunshine, watching his friend. He was amazed to see Bernie charge right over there, so confident.

But Bernie was not at all confident, and the closer he got to her, the more he wondered ... was he doing the right thing? Maybe he should just walk past her and forget the whole thing.

When he got to the bench, Bernie still hadn't made up his mind what to do, so he did what came naturally. He cleared his throat to get her attention and asked, "Mind if I sit down?"

The blue-hatted lady tried to smile, but it didn't work. Turning away, she had to snuffle her nose into her handkerchief, but she did gesture that, yes, he could sit down.

Oh brother, thought Bernie, *I've definitely made a mistake. Obviously she wanted to be alone.* He decided that he'd just sit there in silence; he wouldn't say anything. And then, in the next instant he heard himself say, "Are you all right? Is everything okay?"

The blue-hatted lady didn't answer. She just shook her head no and stared at the tall windows of First Federal Savings across the street and blinked her eyes about a thousand times. Then she turned even farther away, to stare at the marquee of Appleby's Theater, with its huge letters spelling out "Splendor In The Grass."

Bernie waited for her to say something else, but he wasn't even sure if he should be looking at her because, even though it was a free country and everything, who was he to just show up and sit down and start asking questions? He had made a mistake; he should have left her alone.

Just when Bernie decided to return to the Big Scoop, his ice cream cone suddenly reached the critical point, where so much of it was oozing over the sides, and rolling down his hand, he had to take immediate action. Without even thinking about it, he did what he always did: gnawed a hole in the bottom of the cone and started sucking out the ice cream.

The resulting noise brought the blue-hatted lady's attention back to Bernie. "Goodness," she said, her tears gone and an impish smile on her face. "What a marvelous solution. I've lived all these years, I've had hundreds of ice cream cones, and it's never once occurred to me to do that." Then she slapped her knee and laughed out loud.

By that time Alex had straggled across the street and joined them. "This is my friend, Alex Appleby," Bernie told her. "And my name's Bernie Jones."

"How do you do?" she said, reaching to shake the hand of one boy and then the other. She seemed not at all concerned that both their hands were covered with ice cream. She just laughed at the mess and dabbed at it with her hankie. After that the three of them sat on the bench in silence, staring at First Federal Savings and Waldron's Men's Store and the Big Scoop, watching people stroll by.

Then Bernie came up with a good idea. Without questioning either of his bench mates, he crossed the street to the Big Scoop and returned with three more triple-scoop cones.

Alex accepted his without a word. But the blue-hatted lady thanked Bernie again and again, claiming, "This is absolutely the nicest thing that anyone has done for me in a long time." She seemed happy, and she started in on her cone with gusto, but a few minutes later she was crying again and wiping at her nose with her hankie.

"Are you sure you're okay?" Bernie asked her.

"Well to tell you the truth, what I am is lost. Or rather, my *car* is lost. Which is to say, I can't remember exactly where I parked it. I was sure it was here, right by the jewelry store, but I've looked all up and down the street and ..." Instead of finishing her sentence, she sniffed into her handkerchief some more.

“Watch out!” Alex said, pointing to a glob of ice cream that was about to landslide off her cone and onto her hand. The blue-hatted lady quickly slurped it up.

“Really, you boys must forgive me,” she said. “I feel so foolish. All I have to do, of course, is call Charles, and he’ll come and help me find the car and everything will be fine. Poor Charles, these little episodes of mine upset him so. Last time I did this, he told me, ‘Elizabeth I think it’s time you stopped driving.’

“Stop driving? I told him, ‘Charles, I can’t stop driving. I’ve been driving since I was a girl. How will I get to all the places I need to go?’”

She looked at Bernie and Alex, as though perhaps one of them could supply the answer. They both shrugged their shoulders in reply.

“He’s such a dear man,” she said, “but he reminded me that the last time I drove to town, at some point I got rather confused and, well, I tried to retrace my steps, to the various shops I’d been in, but it turned out I couldn’t remember those either. So I sat here, on this very bench, until all the stores closed, and it started to get dark. Perhaps I could have found my car then, there were so few left in the parking lots, but I was just too exhausted. Finally Charles came walking down the street and took me home.” Bernie got a huge lump in his throat. He almost felt like he might cry, but in the next second the blue-hatted lady's cone reached its critical point, with ice cream spilling onto her hand, so she nibbled a hole in the bottom of the cone and noisily sucked out its contents.

With ice cream ringing her mouth, she continued, in a matter-of-fact voice, "You see, the real problem is, if I call Charles ... well, to put it bluntly, that would be the beginning of the end of my independence." She took a deep breath and said so softly, only Bernie could hear her, "I feel so defeated."

When she looked back up at the two boys she seemed almost angry. "Perhaps that doesn't mean much to you boys. Children take their independence for granted, I suppose. Don't they?" she asked Bernie.

He said the only thing he could think of to say, "I think independence is good."

"I do too," she said. "I think it's essential."

"Yeah, me too," agreed Alex.

After that no one said anything for the longest time. The blue-hatted lady contentedly licked her ice cream cone, smiling and nodding occasionally at passersby, apparently no longer concerned about the absence of her car.

Alex and Bernie took turns pointing with their ice cream cones to the line of cars parked on the other side of the street, "Studebaker. Pontiac. Chevy. Ford. Buick."

Then Bernie jumped up and said, "I know! I've got an idea! Let's go on a penny hike!"

"Goodness," said the blue-hatted lady, slapping her knee again. "I haven't been on a penny hike since I was a girl. I didn't know that anyone even knew about such things nowadays."

"Great idea, Bern!" said Alex. "And while we're at it we can look for the car."

"What dear, sweet boys you are," said the lady, rising from the bench and gobbling down the last of her cone. "And smart too! Now let's get a move on. In the words of my dearly departed grandmother, we're burnin' daylight!"

Bernie and Alex jumped up to join her. No one needed to explain the rules to her, and the three of them immediately began their trek through town.

The first toss came up heads, which took them down Chase Street, even closer to the waterfront, where, as they walked along, they watched boats come in and out of the harbor, and families playing on the beach. They took a left at Francis Street, where there were pawn shops and billiard halls.

"This is exciting," said the blue-hatted lady. "Since we don't know where we're going, I'm not really lost anymore." She laughed a genuine laugh and the boys could tell, at least for now, she definitely wasn't feeling defeated anymore.

"So, um, what kind of car do you have?" asked Alex.

GIFT SHOP
OPEN

"I believe it's a blue car," she said. "But then again it might be green."

"Well, what I meant was, what *make* of car is it? You know, like a Ford or a Dodge or an Oldsmobile."

She frowned. "Oh. Well. That I couldn't say." Then she smiled. "But I'm sure I'll recognize it when I see it. And in the meantime, we needn't worry about it. After all, we're on a penny hike. We have no destination. We're just strolling around. That's the beauty of the thing."

By looking at her keys Alex could tell that her car was a Ford, but half the cars in the world, it seemed, were Fords. The boys were pretty sure the blue-hatted lady wasn't even really paying attention to the cars, because, it was obvious, she was much more concerned about having a good time. She gazed into all the shop windows, drawing the boys' attention to various things she thought were remarkable, or beautiful, or what she said were "preposterously expensive."

Several times she told them, this was positively the best way to spend a day, and that from now on, she and her girlfriend Sadie would simply have to start taking penny hikes on a regular basis. It would be good for them both.

Finally the many tosses of the penny brought the three of them to Brown's Hardware. Bernie gazed at it longingly, wishing he were free to walk in and visit his bike for a few minutes. Just then the blue-hatted lady said, "I haven't been in this store for years. Do you boys mind if we go inside and browse around for a while?"

"I think that's a great idea!" said Bernie.

"Me too!" said Alex.

The boys made a beeline for the sporting goods department, while the blue-hatted lady strolled among the housewares.

Approaching the sporting goods, Bernie experienced a moment of panic. He always did, every time he visited the store, because of course there was always the chance that the bike would be gone, sold to someone else. It could be replaced with another one just like it, but still ...

Ah! A wave of relief washed over him, to see that the bike was still there. Then the blue-hatted lady was next to them and she agreed that, yes, it was beautiful, quite a remarkable bicycle. For several minutes Bernie pointed out all its special features, his face beaming with pride.

As soon as they left Brown's Hardware, just one block up the street, the blue-hatted lady pointed to a green Ford station wagon and said, "Here it is. This is my car. I'd recognize it anywhere."

She unlocked the door, settled herself inside, then rolled down the window and said, "I can't thank you enough, boys. Really, I've had a simply marvelous day."

Bernie and Alex thanked her too, though they didn't exactly know what for.

"There's just one more thing I want to say, then I really must be going." She motioned for the boys to come closer. "When you wake up one day, a long long time from now, and find that you're considerably older than you ever thought you'd be, and when you start to forget things, try hard to remember this one thing ..." She leaned her head out the car window. The boys moved in closer. "Independence," she told them shaking her finger with each syllable. "In-de-pen-dence."

Then she started the engine, blew them both a kiss, honked the horn several times out of sheer happiness, and drove away.

The boys stood there, speechless, for several minutes. Bernie felt the same feeling he had earlier, on the first penny hike, like he was just wandering around, and that anything could happen. Which didn't make any sense, because he was standing in one place, and he knew very well what was going to happen next. Finally Alex broke the silence, "Wow, that was really something. Do you think she'll make it home okay?"

"I don't know," said Bernie. "I sure hope so."

The boys walked to the nearest phone booth, outside the Rexall Drugstore, to call home and say they were on their way, then they turned up Lincoln Street toward home. Neither of them said much, though they gave each other plenty of opportunities, just in case.

Finally, when they did begin to talk, it was about dinner, what each family would be having, and what predicament Paladin would find himself in on "Have Gun Will Travel." Then they went back to identifying cars, an activity that kept them busy the rest of the way home.

Neither of them said it, but each time they identified a Ford, they thought of the blue-hatted lady and hoped she had found her way home safely.

Bernie imagined her pulling into her driveway with a big smile on her face, being greeted by her husband, then hurrying to the phone to call her friend Sadie.

"Sadie," she would say, "I've had the most fabulous day, and I have a surprise for you. Soon you and I are going to spend an entire day doing whatever we want, with no plans whatsoever. Because, thanks to my new friends Bernie and Alex, you and I, my dear, are going to go on a penny hike."

It's A Dog's Life

Bernie's dog, Weezer, stood at the big living room window and gazed out at the world below. In the distance he could hear Rex, the terrier that lived next door, and Streak, the big German Shepherd from down the street. They were barking at ... what was it? Weezer strained to hear. A blackbird? No. A cat? No. Aha ... it was unmistakably a squirrel bark. Because he knew how frustrating squirrels could be, Weezer gave out a chorus of yips in sympathy with the other dogs.

"Weezer! No bark!" scolded Mrs. Jones from the kitchen, where she sat at the table, reading the newspaper.

Weezer cut short his last yip and, in turning away from the window, locked eyes with those of the family cat, Dreamer, who was lounging on the back of the couch, her front paws tucked neatly beneath her.

His barking had awakened her from her nap, and Dreamer was not at all pleased. "Must you bark so loud?" she asked him with her eyes. "Can't a girl even get a little beauty rest on her own couch?"

Weezer, who was always fooled by her pretend-politeness, cocked his head to the side in apology. But he was confused; it seemed she was always napping.

Dogs, of course, do not speak the language of cats, which is mostly through purrs, meows, and uncountable eye, ear and tail signals. Nor do cats speak the language of dogs, which is mostly with barks and growls and a variety of tail wags. But dogs and cats do communicate quite well, with their eyes, when they look straight at and send a message to each other, or allow one in.

While Dreamer had the dog's attention, she thought she might as well add a comment or two. "And," she continued gazing into his eyes, "if those nitwit friends of yours think they'll ever catch that squirrel, they're crazy. Squirrels are faster and smarter than dogs. Have any of those dumb mutts ever caught a single squirrel?"

"Maybe yes, maybe no," Weezer told her with a snort, then he glanced away, to let her know the subject was closed.

In no mood to be ignored, Dreamer sprang from the couch and was suddenly in front of him, peering into his eyes.

"For your information, Buster, not a single dog in this neighborhood has ever even gotten close to catching a squirrel. I should know. I keep track of these things. I am the best hunter on the block. All the pets know that." Then she yawned, showing halfway down her throat, which is one of the many ways that a cat is capable of demonstrating scorn for a dog.

In response to her insult, Weezer exhaled a huge sigh and put his head down on his paws. She had always been like this, rude and crude and devious. When he was a puppy and much smaller, many times - the instant the two of them were left alone in the room - she would jump down from wherever she was laying, slink across the room and swipe her claws across the tip of his tender little nose. Oh! He would howl in pain. But when the people came running to see what was the matter, she would be all the way across the room, licking her tail or staring at the wall, totally unconcerned. They had never known the truth, how she had tormented him all the many months of his puppyhood.

When Weezer got too big for the cat to attack him with her claws, she began punishing him in an even worse way. Everyone in the family knew that Bernie was Weezer's human; for that matter, everyone in town did too. They were always together, boy and dog, a perfect match. Dreamer, who had never chosen any particular human as her favorite, now made it her campaign, to get Bernie to pay attention to her. When he came home from school, she would awaken from her nap, follow him around the house, meowing softly, to let him that know she had been awaiting his return all day, which was not at all true.

The instant he sat down, she would jump into his lap and start up her motor, purring, purring, purring. "What a nice kitty," Bernie would say, and stroke her fur and scratch behind her ears - exactly the treatment that Weezer longed for, and deserved, because he really had been waiting for Bernie to return. He had missed his human! Dreamer, all curled up on Bernie's lap, would catch the eye of the jealous dog and smirk her smirky smile, then close her eyes and purr even louder. Oh how humans can be fooled by the purring of a cat! Often it is entirely false. Frequently it is a ploy used strictly to torture the family dog.

Now, as the cat sat in front of him, yawning, her mouth wide open, her entire throat exposed, Weezer felt the full impact of her insult. Over the years, he had grown accustomed to her cruelty and didn't let it bother him all that much. But today he felt vulnerable, and when she laughed at the idea of dogs catching squirrels, he had to admit, she was right. Neither he nor Rex, nor Streak, and most certainly not King George (the Cunningham's Chihuahua) had ever actually caught a squirrel. Sometimes they bragged that they had,

and the other dogs pretended to believe it was true, but no ... squirrels, like cats, were just too sneaky and slippery.

"Furthermore," said Dreamer, twitching her tail to get his attention, "it's about time you had a bath. You stink!"

Weezer rolled onto his side so he would not have to look at her. He thought his fragrance was just right, a unique blend of all his many adventures. One sniff of him and any dog could tell his habits and hobbies, his likes and dislikes. That's the way it was meant to be. Why the humans and the cat thought he should smell any other way was a mystery to Weezer.

He stole a quick glance at her, to see if she had read his mind, another unique ability of cats. But Dreamer was busy with something else. At that moment she was in midair, jumping to catch a fly that buzzed along the window.

Chomp! She got it on the first try. She mangled it in her powerful jaws and quickly gulped it down. Then she smiled a self-satisfied smirk and daintily licked her paws. "You really ought to try a nice juicy fly sometime," she advised him, with a flicker of her whiskers. "They're simply delicious. A wonderful snack for a spring afternoon." Then she leaped away, back to the couch, before he could remind her of what they both knew: that first-of-the-season flies were always slow and easy to catch. Even a dog could get them. A wave of exhaustion washed over Weezer. He grew tired, very tired. He shut his eyes and within moments was carried away, to a beautiful place that was blessedly cat-free. There were bones in every yard and children running all over the place, the kind who like to throw sticks from morning until night.

Then came a screech that sliced right through his beautiful dream, causing Weezer to jump to his feet. It was his old enemy, the vacuum cleaner. Mrs. Jones, the main human during the day, was pushing the machine back and forth, back and forth, oblivious to its terrible, high-pitched whine. It hurt his ears! He hated it!

So did Dreamer, who glanced up at the sound of the machine, her muscles taut and ready to spring at the slightest sense of danger. But, unlike the dog, Dreamer was able to disguise her feelings and under no circumstances would she ever let him see her suffer. She lived by the cat code of conduct, at all times maintaining a facade of complete confidence, composure and indifference.

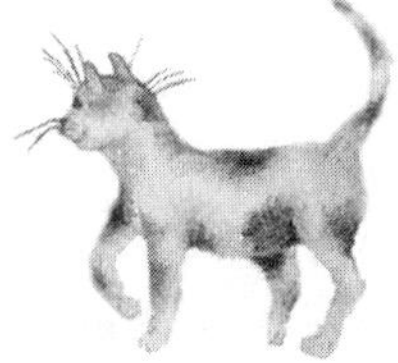

She locked eyes with the dog and said, "Too bad you're not feline, like me. Then you could do all the things you like, all day long. I never let anyone or anything disturb me. Ever. If you were as beautiful and fluffy as I am; if you were the center of the entire family's attention; if you could run and jump and catch as many tiny creatures as I am capable of catching, you would require beauty sleep too." Then she contentedly closed her eyes and began purring, the old chant she had learned as a kitten: "Dogs are dumb, cats are purrrrrfect, dogs are dumb, cats are purrrrrfect."

That's it, Weezer decided. He jumped to his feet, went to the front door and barked furiously until Mrs. Jones opened the door and let him out.

Ah! Freedom! He loved it! He dashed into the spring afternoon, completely cleansed of his encounters with the cat and the noisy machine. Once again the day was new, and off he went, to see what the neighborhood dogs were up to.

The squirrel commotion was over for the time being, and Streak, the German Shepherd from down the block, was now digging a hole in Mr. Cornelius's apple orchard. Weezer stopped and gave him a little yip, to ask what he was doing.

"Oh, just diggin' a hole," Streak answered with an abbreviated bark.

"Buryin' somethin' or diggin' it up?" Weezer asked.

Streak stopped, let his tongue flop out the side of his mouth, and answered honestly, "Gosh ... ah'm not sure, ah guess ah'm just ... diggin." To Weezer or any other dog, it was a perfectly reasonable answer. It was enough just to dig; you didn't need to know why. Anyway, Weezer was only asking to be polite. Streak went back to his work and Weezer went on his way.

Rex, the terrier that lived next door, was sitting attentively on his porch, watching the swallows that flew in and out of the birdhouse. Rex was by nature a barker, and since his family was gone for the day, he took this opportunity to bark at each and every bird that flew by. Weezer felt the urge to stop awhile and bark in sympathy, but he kept going, his tail held high, his nails click click clicking on the sidewalk. Suddenly he stopped and listened. It was the Cunningham's Chihuahua, King George, barking out the news: he had captured a squirrel!

This I gotta see, thought Weezer, hurrying for the Cunningham's yard. There was little King George, at the base of the spruce tree, furiously barking and running, running and barking. Weezer glanced up and saw the offender, calmly perched on a branch near the top of the tree, staring with its unblinking eyes, protectively clutching a spruce cone.

"What'cha gonna do with 'im when ya get 'im?" asked Weezer, forgetting that squirrels were uncatchable.

King George stopped barking and, with a swish of his tail, answered, "I dunno. Eat 'im, I guess."

"Will you save me a bite?" asked Weezer.

"Sure," King George replied.

Pleased with this response, Weezer joined in the barking, and the charging of the tree, and it was blissful. A perfect way to spend half an hour.

But not for all the neighborhood creatures. Mr. Cunningham, who worked the night shift at the paper mill, was at that moment trying to sleep. He pulled his pillow over his ears. Darn those dogs! He had warned King George several times already, and now there was another mutt in the yard.

He opened up the window and yelled, "Shut up Georgie or I'm taking you back to the pound!"

The dogs, even though their knowledge of the human language was limited, did understand "shut up," so they quieted down for a moment. Then the squirrel hopped to another branch and Weezer suddenly remembered that when they caught it, he would get a bite of the furry beast. That inspired him to start barking again. King George, not to be outdone, increased his volume. In a few minutes Streak and Rex showed up in the yard.

King George, because this was his yard and therefore his squirrel, pretended he was trying to run all three of the other dogs off, growling and nipping at their paws, when in fact the dogs were all the best of friends and he was delighted to have their company. Oh how they loved this game! They could play it for hours and hours and hours.

Mr. Cunningham finally reached the point that he knew he would never get any sleep unless he took some action. He shook his tired head, reached for the phone, dialed the Jones's number and said, "Margaret, I think you'd better come and get Weezer before I take him to the pound along with my dog and these two others."

"Oh dear," she said, "I'm sorry. I'll be right there."

The party was great while it lasted. The dogs had as much fun as it was possible to have until the humans showed up. Rex and Streak were shooed out of the yard by Mr. Cunningham, who then tied King George to his doghouse and told him, in no uncertain terms, that he had better be quiet. As soon as Weezer saw *his* human, he made himself as small as possible, tucked his tail between his legs and prepared for the worst. When she shouted out a word he understood, "STAY!" he pretended he didn't know what it meant, and as fast as his legs could carry him, he ran for home.

He waited patiently on the top step. By the time Mrs. Jones got there, with the warmth of the sunshine and the fresh smell of spring in the air, Weezer had forgotten why she was outside in the first place. He sat up, hoping that maybe they were going for a walk.

Mrs. Jones marched up the steps, shook her finger at him and exclaimed, "Bad dog! Now, into the house and no more barking!" Weezer slunk inside and hurried for the living room, for the safety of his oval rug. There he circled three times before settling himself down to lick the mud from between his toes.

"What's this!" Mrs. Jones said, entering the room. "Mud all over the carpet! I just cleaned in here! Weezer ... sometimes you are so dumb!"

"Dumb" was another word that Weezer understood, and he winced when he heard it. Usually on his rug he was immune to criticism or complaint, and he could sleep, or lounge, or just listen to the family, utterly unperturbed by anyone. But not today.

As soon as the unhappy human stalked out of the room, Dreamer jumped down from the couch, stretched herself out to twice her normal size, and strolled over to the rug. She stopped directly in front of Weezer and told him with a glance, "You really are dumb, you know. I am superior to you in every way. I make all my own decisions. I come and go as I please. I am not dependent on the humans for anything. Oh sure, I allow them to stroke me and hold me, but the instant I grow tired of them, off I go, to do whatever I please. I even have my own door. You, on the other hand, must stand and wait for the humans to let you in and out. When you annoy them, they yell at you, and you react in shame. When they yell at me, I go into the other room and scratch the furniture."

Her speech was interrupted by the roar of the vacuum cleaner, pushed by the angry human, down the hall, headed straight for the oval rug. Thinking he was safe, Weezer didn't jump up until the very last second, when the hideous machine was practically on top of him. He scurried to the far corner of the living room and, with each step he took, left another clump of mud.

"Weezer! Stop!" yelled Mrs. Jones, but with the whine of the machine, and the chuckling of the cat, Weezer could not possibly stop. Back out of the room he ran, to the quiet of the kitchen, where the enemy machine never followed.

Just then the back door opened and in came the young human, and everything that was bad became good again. Bernie threw down his books and his lunch bag and ran to embrace his dog. "Weezer!" he said. "How you been, boy? Have you been having a good day?" Weezer's tail began to wag. To see the boy so happy, so enthusiastic, totally erased from his mind the bad thing that had just happened.

"Keep that dog out of the living room, Bernie!" hollered Mrs. Jones. "In fact, I'd like you to give him a bath. He's covered with mud and he stinks to high heaven!"

Bernie, who loved his dog in every possible way, except for occasionally having to give him a bath, filled the big galvanized tub in the laundry room with warm water and dog shampoo. He would much rather be outside playing but, as his mother had reminded him on many occasions, this was part of having a dog.

Weezer observed his young human and suddenly understood the boy's actions. This exact thing had happened many times before. Soon he would be in water ... too much water! Sure enough, a moment later Bernie was calling him, in that tone of voice that meant something bad was about to happen. Weezer plopped his rear end down and stubbornly refused to move. Bernie sighed, for he understood Weezer's reluctance to bathe, and walked slowly toward his beloved dog. Weezer put his head down and, with all his might, concentrated his weight into his lower unit, requiring Bernie to pull him by his collar to the tub. Once he was in the water, with Bernie scrubbing him and calling him a good dog, good dog, good dog, it wasn't really so bad. It was actually kind of fun. For a while.

But, as always, midway through the bath, Weezer was seized with a restless spirit, a sudden unstoppable urge to leap out of the tub and wring himself out with an enormous shake. With water and suds flying everywhere, and Bernie desperately lunging toward him, Weezer bolted from the room. He ran through the kitchen, through the living room, up the stairs, and into Bernie's room, where he crawled on his belly under the bed. Whew, safe at last! So many things had happened today and, though Weezer couldn't recall them all, he was pretty sure most of them had been bad.

Downstairs there was still a lot of commotion going on, which made Weezer tired, very tired. He closed his eyes and drifted away.

Charmaine, who had stopped at a friend's house down the block, was just now entering the house. She scoffed at Bernie's predicament: all that water he had to clean up. He and Weezer were two of a kind: always in trouble.

Charmaine's day at school had been long and hard, and now she was in the mood for some fun. She pranced into the living room, took one look around, spied the cat sleeping on the back of the couch, and decided she would play dress up with Dreamer. "Here kitty kitty kitty," she said sweetly, dangling a piece of yarn on the floor.

Dreamer awoke and instantly focused on the twisting, wriggling piece of yarn. Though she was smarter than the average cat, and a genius in her own mind, Dreamer always fell for the yarn trick. She watched it carefully for a moment, then leaped from the couch and followed it, up the stairs and into Charmaine's room. As soon as she was inside, click, the door closed behind her, and the girl was picking her up, and ... what's this? She was pulling something over her head, and forcing her paws into two tiny holes.

"What a pretty kitty!" Charmaine held the cat up, so she could admire herself in the mirror, wearing a pink dress and a matching pink hat.

"Raaaaer," warned the cat.

"Does the nice little kitty cat want to try on another outfit?" Charmaine asked.

"Raaaaer," the cat replied.

Charmaine knew the game was over. "Oh all right," she said and opened the door. Dreamer ran down the hall and ducked into the first room she came to: Bernie's. Quick, under the bed she ran.

And so it was that Weezer awakened from his nap to a sight he had never seen before: a fully clothed cat.

This was simply beyond imagining for Dreamer. What was *he* doing here? She stood nose to nose with him, embarrassed and humiliated.

He cocked his head to the side and asked her with his eyes, "What are you doing with clothes on?"

She gathered her wits and answered, blinking as calmly as she could, "I am wearing them because I want to. And as soon as I don't want to wear them anymore, I will take them off."

Because he was a trusting sort of dog, Weezer believed what she said, but he was confused. If she liked wearing the clothes, then why did she immediately scurry back out from under the bed and begin wrestling them off?

Undressing proved to be an enormous struggle, and Dreamer was furious that the dog was there to witness it. The hat came off easily enough, but in order to get the dress off she had to roll around and around on the floor and kick savagely with her hind legs. The instant it was off, however, she began serenely licking her paws, to show Weezer that in no way had she lost a shred of her dignity.

Weezer, unblinking, watched her go from wildly battling her clothes off to calmly grooming her multi-colored fur, and though he tried to understand her actions, he could not. Well, cats are a curious thing; Weezer had always known that. But still, he'd have to ask the other neighborhood dogs if any of them had ever seen a cat wearing clothes. He lay his head back down and almost immediately he heard King George barking his unmistakable squirrel bark. Weezer exhaled a happy sigh.

Having once again forgotten that squirrels are uncatchable,

he drifted back to sleep with two comforting thoughts: that if Georgie was able to trap the beast, maybe he would remember to save him a bite. And that, when next he opened his eyes, he would be the thing he knew himself to be ... a good dog, good dog, good dog.

The Haunted House

Bernie and Alex liked to think that because they were Blazing Bandits, they were in on all the big boys' adventures, but that was not the case. They were not included the day the big boys hiked into Peabody Gulch and discovered the haunted house.

It was early on a Saturday morning and the older Blazing Bandits had hiked well beyond where any of them had ever gone before. They whacked around in the bushes for what seemed like hours, then discovered an old overgrown trail, which apparently hadn't been used for a long, long time.

Clark Olsen, because he was president of the club, lead the way. With a willow stick for a machete, he thrashed through the brush, singing "Battle Hymn of the Republic" and "Anchors Aweigh" and all the other military songs he knew. Clark was almost fifteen and had recently decided that when he finished high school he was going to join the Marines, just like his Uncle Joe.

With this thought in mind, he moved faster through the woods than the other four boys, and had to keep hollering at them, to *hurry it up and get the lead out*, and *what were they anyway: a bunch of girls?*

Brian Shaunessey was second on the trail. Normally he'd be keeping pace with Clark, but he hadn't really wanted to come in the first place. The only reason he did come was, well, the other guys would have given him a bunch of grief if he hadn't. Plus if he'd stayed home, he'd have to mow the lawn. He slapped at another bug and silently cursed his best friend, Clark Olsen.

Somewhere, trailing behind Brian, was Larry Rustalio, who was so sweaty and tired and hungry, he now came to a halt, swiped his arm across his dripping brow and shouted up ahead to Brian. "Hey what's the big hurry? I'm starving! When are we gonna stop and eat?"

It was the Patterson twins' turn to bring treats, and Larry was always curious about the treats. When Brian did not answer, Larry gazed off into the trees and noticed for the first time how big and creepy these woods were. There were a few Evergreens scattered around, but mostly all the trees were giant maples, with huge flapping leaves, so many of them that they completely blocked out the sun.

Another cold breeze blew through Peabody Gulch, which

caused all the leaves on all the trees to wobble and wave and rustle against each other. Such a strange, eerie sound they made, it caused Larry to stop thinking about food and to hurry along the trail in an effort to catch up with Brian Shaunessey.

Bringing up the rear were the Patterson twins, Richard and Robert. All their lives they had been arguing with each other, and today was no exception.

"I did not!"

"You did so!"

"I did not!"

"You did so!"

Neither of them was certain what they were arguing about. It was either who had gotten the most ice cream last night, or who had broken the crystal candy dish on Easter. Both were hot topics and required endless debate.

"I did not!"

"You did so!"

To end the discussion, Richard, as he often did, reached out and socked his brother hard on the shoulder, then took off running, while over his shoulder in a singsong voice he mocked, "You can't catch me!" Robert took off after him like a streak.

****

Eventually, all five of the boys were again bunched up on the trail. No one was in a very good mood, except for Clark, who was whistling the "Marine Corps Hymn," and saluting each boy as he came into view. Larry Rusatalio was particularly unhappy because, as it turned out, the Patterson twins had forgotten they were supposed to bring treats. Now there was zero, not one single thing, to eat.

This prompted Larry to throw a big clod of dirt at the nearest maple tree, turn to the Pattersons and say, "Well, whose fault is it anyway? Which one of you guys forgot the food?"

Richard pointed at Robert, Robert pointed at Richard, and at that exact moment Clark Olsen gave a mighty whack with his willow stick, parted the brush, and there, nearly camouflaged by all the bushes and trees, was an old house.

It was so surprising that even Clark Olsen, who always had a smart aleck comment for every situation, was too stunned to speak. When he recovered, he told the others, "Wait here, men."

Thus, Clark got to be first on the crumbly old porch, where he peaked through the broken window panes. This was too good to be true! He turned and hollered to everyone else, "Wait'll you guys see this!"

Then they were all on the porch, trying to see over each other's shoulders, through the cobwebby windows into what was left of the house.

Clark shoved the others out of the way so that he could be the one to open the door and take the first step inside. Just as he reached out to grip the doorknob, though, from out of nowhere, a raven swooped down through the trees and almost brushed Clark's shoulder. It let out a long, loud squawk, circled around the porch, and disappeared back into the forest.

Clark didn't like sudden noises - this one in particular - and in an instant his fear level went from zero to nearly off the chart. Fortunately, he was able to camouflage it by going into a lengthy sneezing fit. Brian Shaunessey, number two in command and always eager to prove himself the best man for the job, wasted no time. He twisted the doorknob and gave the door a shove, which caused it to lunge inward on its hinges. Everyone gasped while the door just swung back and forth, back and forth. Carefully, cautiously, one at a time, the five boys crossed the threshold into the main room of the old abandoned house.

The house was so immediately creepy that Robert Patterson (who, if he'd had a choice, would have given away his entire baseball card collection rather than let the other boys see him cry) started sniffling and whimpering, "Oh man, we gotta get outta here!"

Richard, who was every bit as scared as his brother, only better at concealing it, said, "Oh quit your cryin' ya cry-baby!" Because this, after all, was no ordinary find. They couldn't just run back to the neighborhood and forget about it. It was a whole house, full of ... who knew what? For better or worse, they had to explore it.

"Fan out, men," commanded Clark Olsen. "I'll take this room (he indicated the one they were in). Brian, you and Larry take the upstairs. Richard, you and Robert scout out the other room."

The Patterson twins exchanged a long, anguished look. Then Robert wiped his nose with his sleeve and followed Richard into what must have been, at one time or other, the kitchen.

Brian Shaunessey did not want to obey Clark's command. He did not want to climb the rotting, falling-apart stairs of this creepy, dead old house, but what else could he do? He started for the stairs.

Larry Rustalio was not so obliging. He folded his arms across his chest and said to Clark, "No way!"

"Oh yeah?" said Clark. "Well I'm the boss!"

"Maybe so," said Larry. "But you're not the boss of me!"

"Oh yeah?"

"Yeah."

While Larry and Clark argued and the Patterson twins moved cautiously toward the kitchen, Brian Shaunessey, lean and quick as a cat, crept soundlessly up the stairs. He had one goal in mind: to take a quick look around and hurry back down.

There was only one thing in the upstairs room: an old cedar chest, shoved up against the wall. A streak of light from a tiny window fell onto the center of it, like an arrow, pointing the way. It was obvious to Brian what he had to do.

His heart pounding, his knees weak, he step, step, stepped toward the chest. One quick peak, that's all, he told himself. The lid was heavy, though, so he had to kneel down and put some muscle into the job. Then suddenly it stopped resisting and allowed itself to open, the lid resting against the wall.

Inside there was only a small wooden box, which Brian reached down to open.

As he did, the other four boys appeared at the top of the stairs. For them, the sight of Brian Shaunessey, crouched over the cedar chest, bathed in the strange light from the tiny window, was a sight that none of them would ever forget, as long as they lived. To themselves, the Patterson twins wondered, *how can he be so brave?* Larry Rustalio and Clark Olsen wondered, *how can he be so dumb?*

From the corner of his eye, Brian could see the other boys watching him, so he reached to lift the top off the box. What happened next was forever after a matter of opinion. Clark Olsen claimed that Brian fainted dead away. Larry Rustalio said it was more like a swoon. The Patterson boys said he screamed in terror and threw up his hands and rolled his eyes and slumped to the floor. Whatever he did, in the next instant he recovered from it and scurried on his hands and knees, back to the top of the stairs.

“What?” said Clark. “What is it?”

Brian moved his lips but no sound came out.

Larry Rustalio reached out his hand, to grasp Brian’s, to pull him to where there was safety in numbers.

That’s when Clark decided ... Brian was probably just faking it. There wasn’t anything in the chest. “Come on men,” he said to the others. “Let’s go see for ourselves.”

And so they did, moving together like one enormous person, to gaze down at the contents of the box.

The sound of the four boys screaming was enough to

snap the fifth boy out of his stupor and he, too, joined the chorus. For there, hidden in the depths of the cedar chest, looking quite small and harmless, was a human hand.

The Patterson boys were the first ones down the stairs. Taking them two, three, four at a time, Richard and Robert, shrieking at the top of their lungs, raced toward the door. Right behind them were Clark, Larry and Brian.

All the way down the long, long trail, through the woods, along the banks of Peabody Creek, they ran. They splashed through mud puddles, they jumped over stumps, they sprinted for all they were worth.

And finally, their legs aching, their breath coming in painful gasps, there it was: the trail that lead up the hill and back into the neighborhood.

As if walking into another world, they emerged onto the border of Mr. Cornelius's apple orchard. They could see cars whizzing past on Park Street, and old Mrs. Wolverton across the street, picking lilacs, and three of the neighborhood dogs, furiously barking at a squirrel in a tree. At the Baxter house, several of the neighborhood girls were playing on the swing set.

Clark gestured for everyone to gather around. "All right you guys, no one breathes a single word about this. Got it? What we gotta do now is ... one or two of us have to volunteer to go back down there, and take another look, and make sure we really saw ... what we really saw."

When no one volunteered, Clark pretended to scan his finger randomly at the boys. "In that case, *you're* the lucky guy who gets to go." He was pointing at Brian.

"You're crazy," said Brian, "I wouldn't go back down there if you paid me a million dollars."

Clark tried to bully the other boys, but it was obvious that none of the Blazing Bandits would consider going back down the hill. It may have been the one thing that all five of them ever, in their many long years together as friends, agreed upon: that not even a million dollars could entice them to revisit the haunted house.

Just then, strolling down the alley, whistling a happy song, balancing a badminton racquet on the tip of his finger, came good old Bernie Jones. Ten steps behind him was Alex.

Bernie only caught the words "a million dollars," but that's all he needed to imagine the best possible news.

"You guys found a million dollars?"

The big boys exchanged a glance, and their devious minds simultaneously came up with a plan.

Clark, of course, did the talking. "Mmmmaybe we found a million dollars ... and maybe we didn't. Mmmmaybe we'll share it with you, and maybe we won't."

"Really? You guys really *did* find a million dollars?" Bernie's eyes lit up with glee. Alex, who sensed something suspicious, scrunched up the entire side of his face, so that his glasses would slide into place, and also because he was nervous.

"You two guys prob'ly didn't even know ... there's a big house down in Peabody Gulch," Clark said. "It's been there for a couple hundred years."

"There is not!" said Alex.

"Is so!" said Clark. "And inside that house, upstairs, there's an old cedar chest. Inside the cedar chest there's a little wooden box. And inside the box is a treasure beyond your wildest dreams."

"Wow," said Bernie, "Is that where the million dollars is?"

"Yup," said Clark.

Meanwhile, Brian Shaunessey, for the second time in five minutes, wiggled his left hand around, as though it was completely disconnected from his body. Then, with his right hand, he pounced on the left, and wrestled it into submission. This made the Patterson twins laugh so hard, they both ended up with hiccups. Clark finally settled them down with a long, menacing look. He then turned to Bernie and Alex and told them, "The house is ... mmm .... about a half mile up the creek. But I wouldn't advise you guys going there. It's too dangerous. We're not going back down there again, unless it's with our parents." He solemnly nodded his head at his wisdom. The other four nodded in agreement. And with that, the big boys walked away.

Bernie turned to Alex and said, "We gotta go down there and find that house, and see if there really is a million dollars in it."

"I don't know about that, Bern," said Alex. "Something seems a little fishy to me. Didn't you notice how all those guys were laughing? Is this gonna be another one of those things where we end up making fools of ourselves again?" He peered into his best friend's eyes, awaiting his good judgment.

"I don't know. It could be," said Bernie. "But we don't have anything better to do. Let's go and have a look."

As the two of them were heading down the hill toward the creek, along came Joey Wondermore.

Today was one of the few times Joey had ventured out into the neighborhood. He was closer in age to the big boys, but he had instinctively merged with the two he was more akin with. To Bernie and Alex he hollered out, "Hey! What're you guys doing?"

Bernie told him the story, which caused Joey to burst out laughing. "A million dollars! Ha! That's a good one." What he meant by that, Bernie and Alex did not know.

“Oh well, so what,” Joey said. “It’s a nice day for a hike.” And with that, the three of them continued on into Peabody Gulch.

✲✲✲✲✲✲✲✲✲✲✲

As long as Alex stayed in the middle, he wasn’t too worried about bears or coyotes or bobcats jumping out of the bushes and eating him. But just to be safe, he sang the theme songs from all the television shows he could think of, plus some of his favorite Christmas carols.

Bernie would have preferred a little more quiet on the trail but Alex ... well, Alex was a guy who liked to do his own thing, plus Bernie understood his motivation. Joey still could not comprehend Alex’s need to sing every time they walked in the woods, but he too accepted it and no longer complained.

They reached the place where the main trail dissolved and the non-trail began. It was here that the maple trees became so thick that they pretty much blotted out the sky. Plus there were lots of bushes with stickery, pokey thorns.

“We’ll be lucky to get out of here alive,” said Alex, swatting at a swarm of mosquitoes.

They walked and walked and walked and finally there it was, silent and still and spooky ... the old abandoned house.

Wow! This is really cool!” said Joey.

"Yeah," said Bernie. "I wonder how come we never knew about this place. I wonder who used to live here?"

Alex's heart had begun pounding the instant he saw the place. "Are you guys nuts?" he said. "This isn't just an abandoned house, it's a haunted house."

Joey shook his head and said, "There's no such thing as a haunted house!" In the next instant he was on the porch, calling over his shoulder, "Last one in is a rotten egg!"

Before Bernie could decide whether he should take the advice of his best friend, or go inside the haunted house, he too was on the porch. Alex, because he was too scared not to, trailed along behind. As soon as he stepped inside, he grabbed hold of the back of Bernie's tee shirt, twisted it into a knot and hung on for all he was worth. It was pretty dark inside; the boys could barely see to find their way around. To make it even creepier, with every step they took, the floorboards creaked and squeaked and groaned.

Up the stairs they crept, Joey in the lead, followed by Bernie, who was glad that Alex was so close behind him.

"Do we have to do this you guys?" Alex said. "Can't we just go home?"

Joey and Bernie kept inching toward the cedar chest, then Joey was kneeling down in front of it.

"Man this thing is heavy!"

When it gave way, Joey reached inside for the small wooden box. Both Bernie and Alex clamped their eyes shut, and again Alex hid behind Bernie.

When he opened the box, Joey gasped, then five seconds later, in a perfectly normal voice, he added, “Holy Cow!” He brought the box closer to his face for a better look, then closed it and slipped it into his backpack.

“What is it?” said Alex, still cowering behind Bernie.

“Yeah, ” said Bernie, “we want to see.”

“I’ll show it to you on the trail,” said Joey, jumping to his feet. “But for right now ... let’s get out of here!”

As quickly as they had entered the house, they exited. When they hit the main trail, where the sun was bright and the day was ordinary, Joey brought the wooden box out of his backpack.

“All right you guys, now before I show you what’s in here, you’ve got to understand ... it’s not what you think it is.”

He unzipped his backpack and withdrew the box. “I gotta warn you guys that what’s in here looks very much like a human hand. Anybody would think it is. Only, it’s not. It’s made from some kind of really lifelike plastic, I think.” And with that, he opened the box.

Knowing that it was not what it seemed to be is the only thing that made it possible for Bernie and Alex not to scream. And even so, they both gasped, because the hand looked so real.

Bernie said, "Doggone it, Alex, you were right! The big boys have tricked us again!"

Alex shook his head in disgust. "Those guys are always pulling mean tricks on us!"

"Yeah," said Bernie, "and we're members of their club!"

"You are?" said Joey. "I know what I'd do if I was a member of their club and they did this to me!"

"What?" asked Bernie.

Joey answered him, and five minutes later the three boys hurried back up the hill.

****

The first person they saw was Charmaine, who always knew everything that was going on in the neighborhood. She told them that all the big boys were having a meeting up in Clark Olsen's attic.

According to their plan, Alex scurried to the Olsen's side yard, just below the attic window, and waited while Bernie and Joey snuck around to the back door of the house. The two of them then slipped soundlessly up the stairs and waited for the next thing to happen.

Inside the attic, the big boys were having the time of their lives. They were laughing and making jokes about the haunted house, and how scared Bernie and Alex would be when they found the hand. Brian was still amusing everyone with his dead-hand trick. Not a word was spoken, or ever would be, about the terror each of them had experienced earlier in the day.

That's when Alex, down in the yard, started throwing pebbles against the attic window. All five of the big boys pressed their faces against the glass to see what was going on. When they saw who it was, Clark opened the window and hollered, "Are you guys back already?"

Alex shouted, "Yeah, we went down to that house, just like you said, and we found the wooden box in the old cedar chest. But when we looked inside of it, it was empty." He made sure to look at each of the boys, which was easy to do because their eyes were as big as saucers.

"It was ... empty?" Clark repeated. The Patterson twins, who were quick to panic and who hadn't fully recovered from their earlier fright, clung to each other's arms. A pained look appeared on Larry Rustalio's face. Clark Olsen and Brian Shaunessey exchanged worried glances.

While they were distracted, Bernie had been able to reach out and place the hand just so inside the room, where a person would have to step right over it, to get out. Then soundlessly the two boys sneaked back down the stairs, to join Alex in the yard.

The three of them were almost to the Jones's house when they heard the screams. The Olsen's house exploded with shrieks and screams. The big boys vacated the place so fast, they almost seemed to disappear as they splintered off in five different directions. It was easy for Joey to sneak back in and retrieve the hand. Then he joined Bernie and Alex in the Jones's yard. The three of them climbed trees for a while, then they wandered over to the Appleby's basement, where they played with Lincoln Logs for the rest of the afternoon.

The next day, while they were in the Jones's back yard, staring up at the clouds, Alex said, "Know somethin' Bern? I'm really glad Joey Wondermore moved to our neighborhood. He's not like any of the other big boys."

Bernie said, "Yeah, I'm glad he moved here too. We've only known him a couple months, but he's never once tried to trick us or make fools of us."

And so it was that on that spring day a thing of substance and importance was solidified: a friendship. One that was destined to last a long, long time. One for which Bernie and Alex and Joey would each happily have paid a million dollars.

AUTHOR

Sharon Bushell

Born and raised in Port Angeles, Washington, Sharon Bushell moved to Alaska in 1977. She has been a features writer and columnist for the Anchorage Daily News for many years. Bushell has received numerous awards for her writing, including the Pacific Northwest Excellence in Journalism Award. In 2003 she was honored with the Alaska Governor's Award for the Arts and Humanities for compiling and editing first-person accounts of hundreds of Alaskan old-timers.

In tandem with writing for adults, Bushell has written a series of children's stories whose characters are set in the 1950s. Produced with music and sound effects for local public radio station KBBI, the Bernie stories have aired in public radio stations around the country. They are now in book form as well as CDs.

Bushell's dream is quite specific: for children, parents and grandparents to enjoy the Bernie stories together, to discuss their meaning, and to share their own stories with each other, preferably while sitting close and sipping cocoa.

Sharon Bushell

ILLUSTRATOR

Katie Miller

Katie Miller was born in Homer, Alaska on November 10th, 1990. She is an artist, musician, and active sports enthusiast. In 1998, Miller's drawing of an Alaskan moose won her a blue ribbon at the Ninilchik State Fair... the "Biggest Little Fair in Alaska."

The Trouble With Bernie is Miller's first book project as an illustrator. Her inspiration comes from many places. Her home is situated in a beautiful location, her life is filled with activities, and she has many friends.

One of her teachers describes Miller as happy, hard working and not willing to settle for anything but the best.

Katie Miller

The Trouble With Bernie

Visit Bernie's Website

www.berniejones.com

contests and prizes

Bernie CDs read by Sharon Bushell
with really cool music and sound effects

contact the author and illustrator

and most important............

get a copy of Bernie's next book